# THE TOMBS OF ANAK

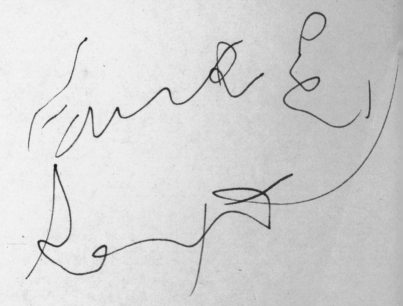

# THE TOMBS OF ANAK

## Frank E. Peretti

CROSSWAY BOOKS • WESTCHESTER, ILLINOIS
A DIVISION OF GOOD NEWS PUBLISHERS

*The Tombs of Anak.* Copyright © 1987 by Frank E. Peretti.
Published by Crossway Books, a division of Good News
Publishers, Westchester, Illinois 60153.

Cover illustration and design by Dwight Walles

First printing, 1987

Printed in the United States of America

Library of Congress Catalog Card Number 86-73183

ISBN 0-89107-442-2

*To the kids at*
*Island Christian School,*
*Vashon Island, Washington*

# ONE

"Hey, listen, I don't need to hear any more foolish talk about ghosts!" said Jerry Frieden with a dusty slap against his thigh. "Dr. Cooper's entrusted this task to us, and I say we just get at it!"

"Nobody's talking about ghosts," Bill White drawled from under the brim of his hat.

"We just don't want anyone to get hurt," Jeff Brannigan tried to explain. "And that goes especially for you."

The three men stood in the middle of an archaeological excavation in a small and narrow valley surrounded by rocky hills. They were wearing brown dust like a uniform; the hot noonday sun was baking their backs. Slow-talking Bill White was the team leader in the absence of their boss, Dr. Jake Cooper. Big Jeff Brannigan was the equipment specialist. Jerry Frieden was the first-time, tag-along, youthful upstart with more ambition than common sense. Their heated discussion was taking place around a man-sized, seemingly bottomless hole in the ground, a hole that hadn't been there ten minutes ago!

"Listen, this is something extraordinary! It could tell us something we never knew about the ancient Philistines!"

"Maybe . . ." said Jeff, not too enthusiastically.

"Well?" Jerry couldn't believe how these guys were dragging their feet. "An incredible archaeological find opens up right in front of us, and you guys are just going to stand there?"

"Well now, just what interest would you have in archaeology? Aren't you and your money-minded bosses interested in something else that might be down there?"

"I say we wait until the Doc gets back," said Bill with a shake of his head.

"It just isn't worth the risk, Jerry," Jeff agreed.

Jerry only grabbed the rope he'd secured to their portable winch and stepped toward the hole. "Suit yourselves. This discovery's going to be all mine."

Bill put a firm hand on Jerry's shoulder. "Listen, you have no idea what's down there. We don't even know where this hole came from."

Jerry only sneered at him. "Spooks, Mr. White, remember?"

Jeff had heard enough of Jerry's taunting. "Now listen here, Mr. Frieden, sir, we're letting you tag along because the big bosses want you here, but you haven't been out on a lot of digs like we have. Most legends are just talk, sure, but behind every one of them is a little bit of truth, and it's wise to pay attention to everything you hear."

"Well," said Jerry, tying the rope around his waist, "I'll buy the stuff we heard about ancient tombs being here—that makes plenty of sense . . ."

"Yeah, but you're forgetting—"

"The *ghost* haunting this place? No sir, Mr. Brannigan, that's where I draw the line."

"Not a *ghost*, you stubborn youngster! That's what the locals talk about, but it could be traps . . . snares . . . vipers! Listen, people *have* been hurt in this place. Dr. Cooper would know more about what to expect down there!"

"Are you two going to lower me down, or do I have to do it myself?"

Jeff and Bill looked at each other, and both were sick to death of arguing with this kid. With sighs and shrugs, Jeff manned the winch and started uncranking the rope as Bill helped Jerry move carefully down into the narrow hole.

"You be careful now, son!" Jeff cautioned.

"Where's your light?" Bill demanded.

Jerry resented the question. "On my belt, Mr. White. Don't worry about it."

"I still have a bad feeling about this," Bill muttered.

Jeff made slow, steady turns on the winch as Jerry worked his way into the hole, one groping foothold at a time, disappearing from the waist down, then the chest, then the head, and finally the hat. Bill stood at the brink of the hole, feeding the rope down and peering after the cocky explorer.

"Get that light on!" he called.

"All right, all right!" came the echoing answer.

Jeff let out more and more rope, and soon Bill could see nothing in the shaft but the occasional sweep of Jerry's flashlight beam.

"How deep *is* this thing?" Bill wondered.

"I've let out forty feet of line," answered Jeff.

Bill hollered down the shaft, "Jerry! Can you see the bottom?"

Jerry's voice sounded miles away as he called back, "Yeah . . . I think so . . . Hey, you guys are going to like this! There's a room down here, and—"

The voice stopped abruptly, and Bill couldn't see the flashlight beam at all now. The rope quivered.

"Jerry?" he hollered.

The rope was still shaking as if it had hooked a fighting fish.

"Jerry!"

Bill heard a scream, some rocks tumbling and clunking, another shrill cry.

"Jerry!" Bill yelled again. He shouted to Jeff, "Haul him up, quick!"

Jeff heaved the crank backward with a groan and gritted his teeth. "He's heavy!"

"C'mon!"

"Bill, he's *heavy!*" Jeff was amazed at how heavy!

Bill ran to help, and they both pulled on the winch with all their weight. It felt like a whale on the other end!

Oof! Suddenly they were both on their backs in the dust. The winch was spinning, squeaking, frantically bringing up yards of loose, flopping rope. They recovered, scrambled for the winch, hauled in more rope.

The end of the rope flipped dramatically out of the hole like a whip and landed right in their laps.

The end was cut neatly. Cleanly.

They scurried to the edge of the pit and shined a light into the blackness; it was like looking down a deep, deep well.

"Jerry!" Bill called again.

Something answered, but it wasn't Jerry. The very sound of it chilled them and turned their stomachs. From somewhere down there, unseen, unknown, a voice, or a siren, or some animal cried out in long, wailing tones that bounced and echoed up the shaft like distant wolf howls—low notes, then higher ones, a definite melody, an eastern, melancholy scale, a mournful dirge that continued note after note after note.

Then the melody faded, dying away far into the depths of the earth, and it was only in the final silence that the men awoke from their horrified stupor.

Jeff looked at Bill and spoke for both of them. "Wait'll the Doc hears about *this.*"


"Doc," a handsome and rugged man with blond hair and probing blue eyes, was in Jerusalem at a large and impressive museum, sitting at a conference table with two important gentlemen who were behaving less and less gentlemanly, and he was beginning to wish he was back at the dig where he belonged.

"I'm not sure I understand your impatience, Mr. Andrews," he said calmly to the man who seemed the most upset. "Archaeology isn't done with a bulldozer. It's a craft of fastidious detail and close attention; you simply can't rush it."

Mr. Andrews, a very cold-eyed, grim-faced man, was proud of his reputation and influence as an international dealer of ancient relics and artifacts, and he wasn't used to waiting for *anything* he wanted.

"Dr. Cooper," he said, his eyes narrow, his face reddening, "you were highly recommended to us as a man who can produce results . . ."

"You got excellent results from the last crew you hired. They unearthed an ancient Philistine temple of Dagon, and that in itself is an incredible find."

The other man murmured in disgust, "Sure, they found it, but they didn't finish the job according to our agreement."

This was Mr. Pippen, a small, nervous man who fidgeted and twitched a lot and was very hard to get along with.

Dr. Cooper asked him, "How could they finish the job when you fired them?"

Mr. Pippen glared at Dr. Cooper for issuing such a challenge. "They were dismissed because they refused to go back to the site. They were a cowardly bunch, afraid of their own shadows, wanting more protection, more money . . ."

"Protection from what?"

Mr. Pippen seemed unwilling to answer. "Have you encountered anything strange or dangerous out there?"

"For instance?"

"Ghosts, bandits, marauders, they said," Mr. Pippen grumbled. "They were cowards."

Andrews cut in. "Dr. Cooper, we're just trying to get something more for our money."

"Well," said Dr. Cooper, "I would say you're getting quite a bit for your money. We've picked up where the last crew left off: we've found the original image of Dagon himself, we've mapped the walls, we've unearthed pottery, papyri, utensils, everything a curator would want."

Mr. Pippen blurted, "But you haven't uncovered *everything!*"

Dr. Cooper looked Mr. Pippen right in his beady little eyes and said, "Meaning, I haven't found whatever it is *you* want, isn't that right?"

Pippen looked away from Dr. Cooper's penetrating gaze and muttered, "We agreed we wouldn't discuss that."

Dr. Cooper waited until Pippen was looking at him again, and then said, "I'm an archaeologist, Mr. Pippen. I'm after Biblical knowledge, something of eternal value. If it's a treasure hunter you want—"

"I said nothing about a treasure!" Pippen snapped.

Dr. Cooper calmly finished his sentence, "—you can keep all your money and hire someone who's after the same spoils you are."

Mr. Andrews stepped in. "Now, gentlemen, this is really unnecessary. Dr. Cooper, yes, I must admit you're doing a splendid job as an *archaeologist*—and really, we couldn't ask for better. It's just that Mr. Pippen has invested a great deal of his money in this project, and I have invested a great deal of my influence and reputation, and we do have our expectations . . ."

"And given reasonable time, I will meet those expectations, *providing* whatever you expect is even there to begin with."

"Oh, it's there!" Pippen insisted. "It has to be there!"

Dr. Cooper had had enough of this conversation for one day. He rose from his chair. "Well then, if I do happen to find *it,* whatever *it* is, you will let me know, won't you?"

Dr. Cooper nodded a farewell, put on his hat, and went out the door, leaving the two businessmen alone to squabble about sellers, buyers, big deals, and money.

As soon as he exited via the big front door, he saw his son, Jay, and his daughter, Lila, excitedly bounding up the museum steps.

"Well," he said, "what happened to all your Holy Land sightseeing?"

Fourteen-year-old Jay, a young man already developing the toughness of his father, looked grim. He handed Dr. Cooper a slip of paper. "This message just came from Gath."

Lila, strong and beautiful at thirteen, made a guess. "I'll bet it's that extra guy, that Jerry. Bill and Jeff never did like having him along."

"Neither did I," Dr. Cooper admitted, unfolding the paper. "Pippen and Andrews couldn't trust us to do the job unattended, I guess . . ."

His voice trailed off as he read the note. He checked his watch.

"Let's go," he said.

They piled into Dr. Cooper's jeep. According to the message, "something" had happened out at the dig. It would be a long and grueling drive, but they could make it back before nightfall.

The jeep roared into the camp above Gath at dusk. Bill and Jeff were there, waiting anxiously for the Coopers' arrival. The extra man named Jerry was nowhere to be seen.

"Is it Jerry?" Dr. Cooper asked, climbing hurriedly out of the jeep.

"We've lost him," Bill reported.

Dr. Cooper grimaced in a way that showed he wasn't surprised and yet was concerned. They all rushed down to the site as Bill told Dr. Cooper everything that had happened, including their discovery of the mysterious pit.

"A *pit?*" Dr. Cooper asked, his eyes narrowing.

"Right behind the altar site," said Jeff.

"I've never heard of any deep excavations under a Philistine temple."

"Well, it sure surprised us," said Bill. "We were cleaning out around old Dagon and got him about half uncovered when this hole opened up. There must have been a very thin lid of stone over the top, and we accidentally broke it and it fell through."

They descended into the narrow valley. Dr. Cooper's crew had accomplished much: they had managed to unearth the original walls of an ancient temple of Dagon, the bizarre half-man, half-fish god of the Philistines. The old doorways were visible, and toward the center, half excavated from eons of sand, rock, and sediment, was the eerie stone image of Dagon himself, staring down at them with a fiery expression.

But all this was of secondary importance to the Coopers and their crew at this moment. They passed it all by and went directly to the spot right behind the fish god to examine that mysterious hole.

Dr. Cooper lay on the ground and shined his flashlight deep into the shaft, carefully examining the walls. He did some scraping, some brushing, and then tossed a pebble in to get some idea of the depth. He was fascinated—and visibly puzzled.

"Any idea what it is?" Bill asked.

Dr. Cooper shook his head. "It doesn't make sense. It *is* man-made, but I've never known the Philistines to be such highly skilled quarrymen and tunnelers."

"So what are we going to do?" Jeff wanted to know.

"Where's that rope?"

Bill found it and handed it to him.

Dr. Cooper examined the cut end. "You're right—it didn't break and it didn't tear. It's cut with a very sharp instrument." Dr. Cooper was distressed about the situation, and it showed on his face. "Did you hear anything?"

Bill and Jeff knew the answer to that question, but they hesitated to say it.

"Uh . . ." Bill started, knowing it was going to sound very weird. "We heard somebody . . . some*thing* singing down there."

That brought the curious look from Dr. Cooper they had expected. *"Singing?"*

All they could do was nod.

"There's no other word for it," said Jeff. "It was creepy, like nothing I've ever heard before."

"Was it a *voice?"*

The two looked at each other, then shook their heads.

"Didn't sound like a voice," said Bill. "Maybe an animal of some kind."

Jeff shook his head. "No, no animal would know a precise melody like that. The thing sang real music, Doc, a real tune."

"What kind of a melody?"

"Well . . ." Jeff tried to whistle a few notes, and Bill tried humming it.

Jay and Lila stood there fascinated. It could have been funny, watching these two men trying to piece together music they had heard, but the melody they were recreating had such a sad, eerie sound to it that the Coopers could feel their nerves tingling.

"Sounds eastern," Lila mentioned. "A minor key."

"Yeah," said Bill, "and then it went up . . ." Again he tried humming it, and again Jeff tried whistling it.

Suddenly Jay noticed another note playing. He could hear *three* melodies, not just Bill's and Jeff's.

"Hey, wait a minute," he said quietly.

Bill and Jeff stopped, but the melody did not. They all stood there silently in the gathering dark. They could all hear it. From somewhere in the rocky hills above them, a melody was playing slowly, mournfully.

"Did it sound like that?" Dr. Cooper asked in a whisper.

"Well . . ." said Bill. "The tune's right, but that's . . . that's a *flute* or something."

"Shepherd's flute," said Jeff.

They listened another moment. The sound was moving slowly along the length of the valley.

"We'd better take a look," said Dr. Cooper.

Bill grabbed his rifle, and Jeff settled for a good-sized club. Dr. Cooper buckled on his 357 revolver.

"Stay with me," he told Jay and Lila.

They followed the sound, which was somewhere in the hills on the east side of the valley, still moving, fading behind the large rocks and then emerging again. Dr. Cooper, Jay, and Lila headed straight for it. Bill moved left, and Jeff moved right. Beneath their feet the yellow grass crunched like a stiff brush, and the broken, jagged rocks made footing difficult. They moved upward, crouching between the boulders, listening for the sound, climbing high above the valley, gradually getting closer. The sound of the flute was still moving, getting further from the dig.

Just then it stopped. The Coopers halted to listen. Nothing.

Then, almost sounding out of place, a goat bleated, and then another. Dr. Cooper smiled a faint smile. He continued up the hill, followed by Jay and Lila. A quick, quiet whistle to the left told them Bill was not far away, and another whistle came from Jeff off to the right.

They found a small trail along the top of the ridge, and the bleating of the goats was very clear now.

The Coopers walked along the path, moving past the towering rocks, looking this way and that, somewhat relaxed. They rounded a corner and saw a small flock of goats playing, meandering, and bleating.

"Ah ha—it must have been a goatherd," concluded Dr. Cooper.

"YAAAA!" came a shriek from above, and before Jay and Lila knew what was happening, a tangled blur of skins, rags, hair, and flailing arms dropped on their father, knocking him to the ground. The kids knew that the assailant—a wild little man, a crazed character with a crude wooden peg for one leg—would be no match at all for their father. But this little guy was sure determined, clinging to Dr. Cooper like an angry cat! Dr. Cooper flipped and twisted with great power, and the man went tumbling head over heels. But Dr. Cooper was barely on his feet before the peg-legged attacker came at him, swinging a staff and still hollering.

"Hey you, hold on!" Jay shouted as he ran near, ready to grab the threatening character.

"Watch that staff, son," said Dr. Cooper, crouching to face the next attack.

The little man swung the staff, and Dr. Cooper ducked as it whistled over his head once, then twice. On the third try, he was able to grab it, give it a yank, and then trip the little man with a well-placed foot.

The strange character went tumbling in the dust, but sprang back to his feet, his eyes full of fight and fear. Then he realized his hands were empty.

Dr. Cooper now held the staff and tossed it to Jay as Bill and Jeff arrived to help. The little goatherd was beginning to realize he was far outnumbered. Dr. Cooper approached him, and he began to back away timidly.

"If you could control yourself for a moment," Dr. Cooper said in a calm voice, "we'd like to have a word with you."

The hairy little man in the goatskins didn't seem too willing to discuss anything. But suddenly finding new courage, he stood his ground and began to rant and rave at Dr. Cooper as if prophesying doom and destruction.

"Invaders!" he wailed, his eyes wide with fear, his finger pointing. "Desecrators! You will be the doom of us all!"

Dr. Cooper noticed a small carved flute hanging from the goatherd's belt. "We heard the song of your flute."

"*The Song of Ha-Raphah!*" The goatherd pointed down the hillside to the dig below. "That is his home. You have invaded it—you have angered him." He smiled a wicked smile and continued, "And one of you has already felt his anger, yes?"

Dr. Cooper had to raise his hand to hold Bill and Jeff back. "How do you know that?"

The little man's eyes widened with awe. "I heard him singing. It means he is pleased, and how can he be pleased but to eat a man?"

Dr. Cooper studied the weathered face for a moment. "He sings that song when he eats a human being? What is he, some kind of animal?"

"He is a *god!*" said the goatherd. "The terror of him fills us all. We serve him or we die." He touched his flute and added, "I played to appease him. If I play his song, he lets me pass."

"And he . . . eats men?"

"Only when he is angry." The little man tapped on his wooden peg. "Once I made him angry." He laughed mysteriously at his misfortune. "Now we have learned to appease him with worship and with offerings, and he does not trouble us." The little man's eyes filled with fear as he said, "But you have angered him, and you cannot appease him. He will devour you—he will devour us all! He is Ha-Raphah!"

Jay and Lila knew the word. "Ha-Raphah," they whispered to each other, "the Fearsome One."

Dr. Cooper asked, "Where can I find him?"

The old goatherd laughed mockingly. "You have invaded his home, so you must meet him—and when you do, you will have no more questions. There is none other like him, and *no one* can stand before him. He fills the earth—he carries the heavens on his shoulders—his might is boundless! Unforgiving is he, unforgiving and cruel, and you will feel the edge of his sword! For you, there is no escape."

"That was a good speech," Bill quipped. "That was very good. You do that well."

"You laugh now," the little goatherd shouted angrily, "but you will feel the terror of our god just as I did!" The man looked at his peg leg again. "I saw nothing, I heard nothing, I expected nothing . . ." Then his eyes narrowed, his voice lowered to a whisper, and he trembled as he recalled, "But it was Ha-Raphah, the darkest of shadows, rising out of the earth without a sound. There was nowhere to flee from him. I felt nothing—only that my leg was gone."

Dr. Cooper and the others were beginning to believe this frightened little man. They could feel their stomachs starting to tighten.

Dr. Cooper finally stepped forward and returned the goatherd's staff. "Go in peace."

"But will you leave his home?" the goatherd asked fearfully, pointing once again toward the dig in the valley.

"Ha-Raphah has taken one of our men. We can't leave without him, even if we have to face your god and his wrath."

"Oh, you will face him, all right," the man said with great assurance. "Remain here, and you will." He took one more look in the direction of the dig. "But not me. No, not me."

He spun and darted away like a frightened bird, herding and shooing his goats along the trail. Dr. Cooper looked at his children and his crew, and then they all looked toward the valley. They knew they had to return, but now they could not help wondering what dangers might be waiting for them.

Without a word, they started walking back.

# TWO

The darkness was settling quickly now. They hurried back the way they had come, stumbling over loose rocks and groping their way along.

"What do you make of it, Doc?" Bill asked.

"Well," mused Dr. Cooper, "what the old goatherd had to say seems to fit all the other local traditions."

"You mean all the tales and rumors about . . . a ghost?" Lila asked.

"Ha-Raphah," said Jay, and he didn't like the sound of it.

"But we have tangible evidence of *something*," Dr. Cooper added. "The loss of the goatherd's leg, our missing man, and that cut rope, not to mention that . . . uh . . . *singing*."

"But . . . a *ghost*?" asked Jeff.

Dr. Cooper thoughtfully reviewed what they had learned from the goatherd. "The darkest of shadows . . . a cruel, tyrannical ghost who eats men, towers to the heavens, sings one melody consistently enough for the goatherd to learn it . . . who inhabits the earth under that dig, who fills the local natives with terror . . . who is revered and worshiped as a deity . . ."

"Now that's some kind of spook," said Bill.

They reached the valley floor just as a golden, glowing moon peeked over the hills and flooded the valley with amber. The hot, dry air lay very still between the hills. The quietness of the night was unsettling.

They had to pass through the unearthed Philistine temple to reach camp, and in the pale moonlight the crumbling walls were starkly lit snags casting long, zigzagging shadows across the sand. Dagon was hideous and ghostly in this light, his face in its own shadow except for his long, limestone nose and his bulging, menacing eyes. Jay and Lila could imagine he was watching their every move.

They were moving through the temple ruins silently, in single file, when suddenly, without a word spoken, they could all feel it: something was wrong. Dr. Cooper quietly froze in his tracks, drew his 357, and held it ready at his side, listening intently. The others halted and stood still. Bill gripped his rifle in readiness.

When some pebbles dribbled down a wall, Dr. Cooper crouched slightly and raised his gun. More pebbles rolled to the earth, and Dr. Cooper waved his children back with his hand. He was looking toward Dagon.

Dagon seemed to be moving. Or was it just the way his shadow seemed to sway, undulate, grow larger?

Jeff stood in front of Jay and Lila, protecting them with his body against . . . whatever it was.

Then they all saw it. It was dark enough to be Dagon's shadow, but it slowly stepped out from behind Dagon, as if Dagon's shadow had broken off and become a living thing, walking like a man.

Dr. Cooper aimed his gun, and Bill threw his rifle bolt into place with a *clack* that broke the silence. Jay and Lila leaped for cover behind the remnant of a wall.

The shadow looked enormous and towered over Dr. Cooper like a tall tree. There was a very tense moment of silence, but the same thought was coursing through every person's mind.

"Ha-Raphah?" Lila gasped.

"Dr. Jacob Cooper?" asked the shadow in a booming lion's growl of a voice. "From America?"

Dr. Cooper didn't lower his gun, and neither did Bill. The archaeologist beckoned with his hand and said, "Step out into the light where we can see you. Identify yourself."

The shadow obeyed and stepped into the radiance of the rising moon.

It was a very large man dressed in dirty tan fatigues and a hat with a wide, drooping brim. He was carrying a very formidable looking rifle, had an ammunition belt across his barrel-sized chest, and looked like some kind of terrorist.

"You were expecting a ghost?" the man asked, and then his big chest quaked with a chuckle. "A visit from Ha-Raphah?" The chuckle stopped abruptly, and the man became very stern. "Had I been the ghost, you would certainly all be dead by now. You should have fired at me when you had the chance!"

"Who are you?" Dr. Cooper asked impatiently.

"The name is Talmai Ben-Arba, of Gath," the man said, offering his gloved hand.

Dr. Cooper thought for a moment, then lowered his gun, shook the big hand, and asked, "And just what is your business here?"

"I would say, Doctor, that you've taken quite a task upon yourself, a task to which you may not be equal. I've been watching your struggles here for some time now, and I think you need another resource. I'm a native of the area, Doctor. I know this place, its moods, its dangers, its superstitions, and its people. I have come to offer my services."

"Well . . . I hope you won't misunderstand," Dr. Cooper said slowly and cautiously, "but the . . . businessmen . . . who hired us already sent us one man to help spur us on, and now he's lost and possibly dead. I can't be responsible for any more tagalongs."

The big man's answer was gruff. "Mr. Jerry Frieden

was, as you say, a tagalong, and he got exactly what he asked for in his foolishness. As for Talmai Ben-Arba, he can look after himself." He added with a glint in his eyes, "As we all must do—isn't that true, Doctor? I understand you have received no assurance of protection or assistance from the government, and your not-so-generous employers, Mr. Pippen and Mr. Andrews, have offered you no favors either, either in equipment or manpower. You, your two men, and your two children are left here to fend for yourselves, yes?"

"And to perform miracles. I'm sure you know that too."

Ben-Arba threw his head back and roared out a laugh that carried into the hills. "Ah, yes, Dr. Cooper, the treasure that Mr. Pippen is convinced is here. You, a Christian man who cares nothing for riches, are now expected to produce a treasure while all you seek is knowledge. Ehh, such is life in the world of . . . business, yes?"

Dr. Cooper called behind him, "Jeff, Jay, and Lila, bring our climbing gear and some lights."

The three went into action.

Dr. Cooper turned back to Talmai Ben-Arba. "You've gone to a lot of trouble to find out about us and our reasons for being here."

"Such information can easily be found by someone who knows the right places to look, the right people to ask."

"So what are you after? You must know I have no money to pay you."

Ben-Arba's voice dropped in pitch, and he spoke as if telling a secret. "I believe in the treasure too, Dr. Cooper. Pippen and Andrews may think they own you, but they do not own *me*, and neither do they own the ground we stand on. Whatever riches may be found will go to the man who finds them, and I intend to be that man. We can help each other: I offer you my knowledge and prowess in exchange for a fair portion of the riches you may find. You will gain knowledge, I will become rich!"

Dr. Cooper sighed and looked at the ground. "*Greed*," he said mournfully. "I think I've seen about all I can stand."

Ben-Arba had no time for little sermons. "What is your answer, Doctor?"

"Mr. Ben-Arba, you're asking for a share of riches that may not even exist. And as for any knowledge and prowess you think you can offer me, you've shown me nothing so far, nor have you shown me why I would even need them."

Just then, one lone, faraway voice like that of a ghostly wolf began to cry out a quiet but mournful tune, a slow and steady succession of notes that rose and fell like a funeral dirge. Dr. Cooper and Ben-Arba froze as the sound reached their ears. Bill held his rifle tightly and listened, watching warily on every side.

Jeff, Jay, and Lila became statues by the supply hut when the sound came to them. Jay and Lila looked at Jeff, and he nodded silently as if to say, "Yeah, that's what we heard."

Dr. Cooper looked at Bill, and Bill spoke very quietly. "Yeah, that's it, that's the sound. But . . . last time it was deep in the ground."

This time it was not underground, but echoing all around them, growing louder, more and more eerie, and ever closer.

As the moon continued to rise and its light turned from dull amber to cold silver, that strange, ghostlike voice continued to wail and lament from somewhere in the dark hills until the melody gave way to a moment of deathlike stillness.

Then, as if on cue, a high and ringing tenor voice from somewhere in the night answered back with a variation of the same song. That voice was joined by another, and then, with more volume, another voice, and then another, and still another joined in the song, carrying it from one end of the valley to the other in waves of anguish, sorrow, even fear. Within a few chilling, hour-long minutes, the voices had become an eerie chorus, singing a lament that filled the valley like a cold wind.

The melody was familiar by now—frighteningly familiar.

*"The Song of Ha-Raphah,"* said Ben-Arba, looking this way and that, listening to the many voices now filling the night air. "Their mighty ghost has called to them, and now they are answering. They are trying to please him."

"Who are *they?*" Dr. Cooper asked, listening raptly.

"His followers. The Yahrim."

Dr. Cooper translated the word. "The Fearful?"

Ben-Arba nodded, his face very grim and his eyes reflecting the silver moonlight. *"He* is the Fearsome, and so *they* are the Fearful." Then he added, "It is the night of sacrifice and worship, but . . . their song has a desperate sound tonight. They are singing for their very lives."

"So you're familiar with Ha-Raphah?"

The big man looked down at Dr. Cooper as a smile appeared on his grisly face. "Some of my knowledge and prowess," he said gloatingly.

"Then please continue."

Ben-Arba's eyes returned to the surrounding hills in wonderment and awe. "They are the people of these hills, a very isolated group of shepherds, goatherds, and traders, with age-old superstitions and a hideous religion that worships Ha-Raphah. This is their land—these are their hills and their sacred places. I don't imagine they—or their god—have ever been threatened by outsiders like us before. In their eyes, Ha-Raphah must be very angry. And I can promise you, no good can come of it."

"How many, would you say?"

"Perhaps three to four hundred altogether, with half of that number armed and dangerous. But they have no modern firearms that I know of. Their religion forbids it."

"Can we negotiate with them?"

Ben-Arba gave Dr. Cooper a look that condemned him for even asking such a question.

"What about Ha-Raphah? Does he exist in any form we'll have to deal with?"

Ben-Arba was impressed with that question. "You are not a skeptic, Doctor?"

"I'm a believer in the God of Israel, in His heavenly messengers, and in *evil* spirits as well."

"Hmmm," Ben-Arba said, still looking toward the surrounding hills. "There is *something* out there, and I do believe in it." Then he chuckled, "But I am also a believer in Talmai Ben-Arba! He can deal with anyone or anything that comes his way."

"Even a ghost?"

Ben-Arba sneered. "Let him show himself, and then I'll decide. We can *all* decide." Then he added, "Which may very well happen if we remain here and continue to tread on Ha-Raphah's ground."

As the eerie music continued to echo around them, Jay, Lila, and Jeff returned from the supply hut with ropes, climbing gear, and lights.

Dr. Cooper beckoned to them to approach.

"This is the rest of the team," he told Ben-Arba. Some quick introductions were exchanged, and then Dr. Cooper pressed on to urgent business. "If you wish to further demonstrate what use you might be, you can appease all these Yahrim so we can go about rescuing Jerry. Regardless of them or their god, we have to go down after him."

"Ehhh, the Yahrim!" said Ben-Arba in disgust. "Let them live up to their name!"

With a swift movement he pointed his rifle into the

air and fired two rounds. The sound of the blasts rang the valley like a bell and broke the chorus of voices into startled disarray. Ben-Arba threw his head back and let out a fierce roar that cut the song short as if with a blade. Now there was a deathly silence.

"Back into the hills with you," he shouted, and the Cooper party could hear the fading sounds of scrambling footsteps high in the rocks.

For a moment no one could think of a word to say. Ben-Arba was glad for that; it made him feel he had impressed them.

"Another sample of my prowess," he informed Dr. Cooper. "And now for another sample of my knowledge: You should think twice before you enter the shaft. The same will happen to you as happened to your pitiful tagalong."

Before anyone could ask what he was talking about, Ben-Arba stepped over to the deep, mysterious hole that had swallowed up Jerry Frieden and shined his powerful flashlight into its bottomless depths.

"It's a ventilation shaft," he explained, "a perfect trap for a full-sized man. You would be squeezed in, unable to move, unable to defend yourself if something should attack you."

"How did you know what it was?" Jay asked.

The big man examined Jay and Lila for the first time, and asked Dr. Cooper, "Why do you bring children to such a place as this?"

"They are quite skilled and competent," Dr. Cooper retorted, "and Jay's question is a fair one."

The dark eyes glimmered with a strange fierceness as Ben-Arba answered, "I will tell you only what you need to know when you need to know it and not before. I have to be sure you will always need me." Then he looked at Jay and Lila again and said, "Doctor, they are *small*."

Jay piped up, "Sure, and that might be a good thing."

He went to the edge of the hole and sized it up. "I'm small, Talmai Ben-Arba, but I'm a fighter, and I wouldn't get stuck in there."

Ben-Arba got a very strange look of glee in his eye as he turned to Dr. Cooper. "Yes . . . yes! Send him first. He will have more freedom to squirm and fight in the shaft. Once he reaches the bottom, he can look out for any dangers and warn you."

Dr. Cooper was about to object, but he held his peace and considered the idea carefully.

Jay and Lila just stood at the edge of the pit and shined their lights into it. It *was* a tight little hole.

Dr. Cooper asked Bill and Jeff, "What was it Jerry said right before you lost him?"

"Something about a room down there," said Bill.

"And then?"

"Something must have grabbed him," said Jeff. "And it was big. We could feel the weight on the rope."

"Ha-Raphah," Ben-Arba said simply.

Dr. Cooper joined Jay and Lila at the edge of the shaft, looked down into that deep, dark well, and then asked them, "Well, what do you think?"

"It might be okay if you send a lantern down first," said Jay. "That way I can see what's below me."

Bill was ready to try it. He prepared a propane lantern on a long rope and started lowering it down slowly. They all watched it descend foot by foot, clunking against the walls of the shaft occasionally and casting a ring of light around itself.

When Bill had let out forty feet of line, he announced, "This is where we lost Jerry."

The lantern was a tiny point of light with a halo around it, swinging slowly back and forth, clunking against this wall and then that one. Bill let out more line, and the halo disappeared.

"And there's the room he mentioned," said Dr. Cooper.

Ten more feet. The line went slack.

"We've hit bottom," Bill reported.

Dr. Cooper lay on the ground with his head over the hole, listening. Jay did the same. There was no sound from below.

Bill had a harness and rope ready for Jay.

"Don't make any unnecessary sound," Dr. Cooper instructed. "If there's any sign of trouble, don't waste any time—holler and we'll pull you up. If things look all right, signal us with your light."

Jay was ready. But something else had to happen first. Without anyone having to say anything, Jay, Lila, Dr. Cooper, Bill, and Jeff joined hands around the mouth of that pit and prayed, as they always did when they felt an adventure beginning. Without the Lord's constant protection, no attempt such as this would ever be made by any of them; that was Cooper expedition policy.

Dr. Cooper finished the prayer by saying simply, "Dear Father, protect Jay, my son. Protect us all. In Jesus' name, Amen."

"Amen," they all said.

"Let's get on with it," Ben-Arba prompted.

Jay was ready. Bill and Jeff manned the winch and started letting the rope out as he stepped backward into the hole, finding a foothold, then another, slipping out of one, refinding it, dropping down into that vertical tube of rock. Ben-Arba was certainly right about the tightness of this hole. Jay could spread his elbows and touch either side of the shaft easily. If a person never had claustrophobia before, this would be an ideal place to get it, he thought.

The dry, limestone walls kept passing by as the air started getting musty. Jay could smell old, earthy smells coming up from beneath him, carried on a steady, cool, upward draft. He kept his light pointed below him, warily looking for anything that could alert him of possible danger. So far, there was nothing to see but the sheer walls of the shaft, and nothing to hear but the gritty sounds of his feet against the rocks.

Twenty feet down, then thirty, then forty.

His pulse quickened. Below him, the narrow walls of the shaft opened into a dark, cavernous space. He could see the lantern resting on the rocky floor far below. It did look like some kind of room down there.

He signaled for a stop with his light, then curled his head down to have a look.

He knew he had to be quiet, but he could hardly contain a cry of excitement. The lantern resting on the floor was illuminating a chamber about ten feet wide and . . . it was hard to say how long; it just stretched out into darkness in both directions. The walls were smooth, as was the floor, now littered with sand and rocks that had fallen from the shaft, perhaps broken loose by Jerry Frieden's struggle. Then Jay saw something on the far side of the passage: a large, smooth slab of stone with very odd writing of some kind. Perhaps his father would be able to read it.

Okay, he thought, now for the next step. He gave another signal with his light and swung his body over the opening as the crew above slowly lowered him into the room. As he hung there in space, slowly rotating and descending, he remembered very vividly Bill's words: "This is where we lost Jerry."

His feet came to rest on the cool stone floor, right next to the lantern. The rope went slack, and then tightened up again. They were keeping a firm hold on him, for which he was grateful.

*Be quiet now,* he thought to himself, *don't breathe too loudly.* He listened for a moment. Except for the mournful sighing of air moving up through the shaft, there was no sound louder than the beating of his heart. He forced himself to look all around. He had to know what was in the room, good or bad, like it or not.

His search ended abruptly as his wide eyes fixed on

a single object on the stone floor—a shoe, torn open and tossed aside.

Then his eyes caught the sight of another object just at the edge of the lantern's circle of light. It was a tool . . . a small pick. It was Jerry Frieden's.

Now he was scared.

# THREE

Jay forced his eyes to sweep in a wide, slow circle all around the cold, dark, mysterious room. Except for the shoe and the pick, the room looked empty, and Jay couldn't see any door in or out. There were relief carvings on the walls—carvings of warriors, battles, and pagan deities. The figures were gruesome and monstrous, their exploits gory and violent.

Another moment passed. He could see now that this chamber was not a room but a hallway, a tunnel. There was no telling how far it went in either direction. Jay's curiosity was gradually overcoming his fear.

Well . . . the crew above was waiting. Jay slipped out of the harness, then pointed his light upward and waved it back and forth. A moving light above indicated they had seen his signal. The harness went back up the shaft.

Dr. Cooper secured the harness around himself and stepped into the shaft. With silence and caution, he disappeared into the hole as Jeff manned the winch.

It was a tight, eerie place, and Ben-Arba was right—it was a dangerous place for a full-sized man to be trapped if something wanted to attack him.

Ten feet down, fifteen, twenty. He carefully examined the ancient tool marks in the limestone. The quarrymen had worked with great precision and skill. The tube was perfectly round, and its walls were exactly vertical.

At forty feet he reached the ceiling of the room and dropped into the open space below. Jay was there standing guard, his eyes wide open, his light sweeping about. As Dr. Cooper's feet touched the floor, he looked at Jay, and Jay responded in a hushed voice, "All's quiet." Then Jay pointed out the shoe and the pick with the beam of his flashlight.

Dr. Cooper got out of the harness and waved his light across the opening. The harness started back up again. Then he stood there in the middle of the room, almost going through the same little precautions Jay had gone through. He listened for a long time and looked all around the room, shining his light everywhere. He took a very close look at the shoe without touching it, and then the pick. He looked at the relief carvings. He examined some of the inscriptions. He even stooped down and ran his finger across the floor. He was fascinated but very, very puzzled.

"It's all wrong," he said quietly, his voice echoing off the stone walls.

"What's wrong?"

"It appears to be a tomb, but . . . For one thing, it isn't Philistine, and for another thing, it hasn't been deserted."

Jay had sort of noticed that detail, but now he thought about it. The floor was clean, and so were the walls, and that was not at all typical for an ancient, unexplored tomb.

"Then . . ." Jay thought aloud, "someone's been here."

"And quite regularly. Whoever Jerry encountered has inhabited this place for some time, and has done a very fine job of maintaining it."

"So whose tomb is it?"

Dr. Cooper moved over to the smooth slab that

bore the ancient inscriptions. He pored over the intricate characters line by line, trying to make sense of them. He finally shook his head, perplexed.

"The letters are familiar, but . . . they don't make sense. They don't spell any words I can figure out."

Jay came closer to see what his father was looking at. "Are there some letters missing, or am I just imagining things?"

"There are letters missing, and even whole words, like some kind of puzzle. See here? A letter, and then a gap, and then another letter, and then a whole word. And look—they're arranged according to some kind of pattern, maybe an acrostic—each line begins with the same letter, and then the lines crisscross for some reason."

"Yes," said Jay, "kind of like a crossword puzzle. I wondered about that."

"I think this part down here must be an epitaph of some sort. These are names here, and these paragraphs that follow must be their life histories, perhaps their exploits."

"Some exploits," said Jay, looking at the carvings again.

Dr. Cooper took a closer look at the carvings. Even he was disturbed at the horrible sight. "An incredibly warlike people . . . vicious . . . absolutely savage."

"They didn't have much respect for human life, did they?"

Dr. Cooper shook his head with disgust. "Jay, it's a perfect example of man's sinful nature without God. That's why the Lord commanded Joshua to drive out all the ungodly inhabitants of the land. He didn't want His people coming into contact with this kind of moral and spiritual pollution."

"But . . . who were these people?"

Dr. Cooper kept poring over the carvings and inscriptions. "Well, Canaanites of some kind, but exactly which kind we have yet to figure out." He looked at the strange, puzzlelike inscriptions again, and his eyes suddenly narrowed. "Oh, oh . . ."

"What?"

Dr. Cooper took a small brush from his belt and swept at the letters. He scratched at the stone with the edge of a small scraping tool. "This part up here . . . the part that looks like a puzzle . . . It isn't an ancient inscription. As a matter of fact, it's been made quite recently."

Lila was the next one to arrive in the mysterious chamber, and then, squeezing his way down inch by inch, growling and struggling, came Ben-Arba. He was a big and powerful man, but now his size was a drawback, not an advantage, and he had to shed his weapons before he could even fit in the shaft. As soon as he arrived, disgruntled and nervous, he waved his light across the opening and mumbled, "Be quick about it."

His rifle and ammunition belt followed after him very quickly.

Lila, too, was fascinated and horrified at the carvings on the walls. "Do you suppose Ha-Raphah is like one of *them?*"

Ben-Arba was never one to bring comfort. "He *is* one of them, to hear the Yahrim tell it. They say his den is lined with the heads of his enemies . . ."

Dr. Cooper cut off such talk with a quick question. "Do you know where we are?"

Ben-Arba looked about the passageway both with fascination and a very definite dread. He held his rifle ready. "According to the local traditions, we are in the tombs, Doctor."

"Whose tombs?"

"There are local legends of horrible monsters, vicious giants, fearsome warriors . . . Take your pick. Ha-Raphah would call them all his family, I suppose."

"I take it the Yahrim spend a great deal of time down here?"

"At one time they did. They are very skillful in cutting stone and tunneling under the earth, and I am sure many of these passages and the shaft we came through were carved by their hands. But this has become a sacred place for them now, the home of their god. Only the holy men, chosen by Ha-Raphah himself, can enter here."

Dr. Cooper took a good, long look at Ben-Arba. "Just how much do you really know about this place?"

Ben-Arba only smiled a wide, white smile and answered, "Not everything, Doctor."

Dr. Cooper shined his light down the passageway. He could barely see that the passage turned a sharp corner far ahead, almost invisible in the darkness.

"How extensive are the tombs? Any idea?"

"I believe this is only one passageway of many. Word has it that tunnels stretch for miles within the hills here—up, down, in all directions." Ben-Arba added a solemn note: "Anyone . . . any*thing* . . . could live down here and never be discovered."

Dr. Cooper picked up the lantern. "Jerry's shoe and pick fell this way. Let's have a look."

He went first, Jay and Lila followed, and Ben-Arba guarded from the rear. Step by careful step, they made their way down the cold, musty passage, their lights sweeping here and there, illuminating the high, vaulted ceiling still stained with the soot of ancient torches, and then lighting up the walls, revealing additional carvings of horrible, bloody deeds. Warfare and conquest seemed to be the passion of these people, whoever they were.

Dr. Cooper stopped short.

"What is it?" Lila asked in a near whisper.

Dr. Cooper shined his light toward the floor.

"Jerry's flashlight," he said.

There it lay, shattered and bent.

Ben-Arba came up behind them and hummed a gravelly "Hmmm . . ." Then the white teeth appeared.

"I would say we're going the right direction. Lead on, Dr. Cooper!"

But Dr. Cooper didn't move. He stood there silently, his eyes shifting about. He was listening. They all listened.

Somewhere ahead of them, somewhere in that inky blackness, several male voices were singing a low, droning chant.

"There's somebody down here," said Lila.

"The Yahrim holy men," said Ben-Arba, "in the middle of their secret rites. We've come at a bad time, I'm afraid."

Dr. Cooper extinguished the lantern and left it on the floor. "Jerry's down here too." He used his flashlight instead, keeping the beam low. "Let's go. Quietly now."

They could not see around that sharp corner in the passage, but they could tell the sound was coming from beyond it. They drew closer, and now they could notice a dull, orange glow on the stone walls.

The singing stopped, and Dr. Cooper froze there in the passage, clicking off his flashlight. The others did the same. They stood there in the dark—there wasn't a sound. They waited another long moment. That orange glow had to be some kind of fire. Dr. Cooper clicked his light on again and continued forward.

They came to the corner and slowly moved around it. The orange glow was stronger now, almost enough to light their way. All the flashlights clicked off. Just around the corner was a doorway big enough for a truck to drive through. Dr. Cooper examined all around the door and then leaned inside; Jay and Lila stuck their heads in to have a look also.

They were all silent for a moment, unable to find words to express their amazement at the sight before them: a huge, circular room with a large firepit in the center. A bonfire was burning in the pit, a column of smoke rising to an open vent in the high ceiling. Around the walls of the room were shelves of rock that held a vast assortment of weapons, tools, and armor, as if the room was a bizarre museum.

But the sight that made them all stop in their tracks was right across the room from them, standing against the wall like a gruesome guardian: a large and fierce-looking idol with a man's body and a hawk's head, covered with furs and feathers and holding a very large spear in its clawed hands. It was motionless, but it almost seemed to be alive; the piercing yellow eyes in the hawk's head appeared to study them as if they were a tempting meal.

The hawk-god wasn't alone. There were other idols standing against the walls all around the room, illuminated by the eerie, flickering light of the bonfire. They were man-sized images of birds, beasts, pagan gods, and monsters, and every one of them was holding a very deadly-looking spear in its clawed hands.

"A ceremonial room," said Dr. Cooper. "A place for pagan rituals, I suppose."

"And they have filled it with the weapons of their savage god," said Ben-Arba.

Dr. Cooper listened and looked all around the room from where they were standing. "There's no one here. Whatever they were doing, I think we just missed it."

Dr. Cooper began to step inside the door when Ben-Arba held him back with a powerful hand on his shoulder.

"Uh, Doctor," he said, "do look for spiderwebs."

With that, Ben-Arba nodded at Dr. Cooper to continue.

There were very large, stone steps going down into the room. Dr. Cooper took each one with great caution as the others followed.

The nearest rock ledge held a collection of ancient

weapons. Jay approached it to examine a wicked-looking sword, all the more gruesome because it was at least as long as he was tall. The pattern of the curved blade was familiar. They'd seen the same kind of sword in the carvings they'd passed.

"Look at that spear!" Lila exclaimed.

"What spear?" Jay asked. "Oh, you mean this pole . . ." Then he realized the "pole" was the shaft of the spear. His eyes followed the shaft down to the spearhead, a massive, razor-sharp point of iron that had to weigh twenty pounds.

Ben-Arba groaned as he hefted a huge battle-ax almost as big as he was. "Ah, to go after Ha-Raphah with one of *these*," he said. Then another thought occurred to him that quickly erased the smile from his face. "Or to have Ha-Raphah use it to come after *me* . . ."

"Dad . . ." Jay reflected with great amazement, "these people were *giants.*"

"Definitely," said Dr. Cooper. He was on the other side of the room, examining a very large bone he'd found lying on a table of rough-hewn timbers. "If I'm not mistaken, this is a femur, a thigh bone."

They gathered around to look.

"I think it's on display here, like a sacred object," Dr. Cooper noted. "Let's not touch it." He took a small tape measure from his pocket and measured the bone's length. He then compared the length of the bone to the length of his own leg. The tape measure reached from his hip to his midcalf.

"Are you sure it's human?" Lila asked.

"I'm sure," said Dr. Cooper. "I don't want to believe it, but I'm sure, and now I'm getting an idea who these people were . . ."

Unfortunately, Dr. Cooper didn't have time to continue. There were many shadows in this room, and one shadow had fallen in just the right spot to keep Jay from seeing *a spiderweb:* a very thin, almost invisible, hairlike strand of fiber that stretched just in front of the table at knee-level. He didn't move very far, only half a step, but far enough to press against it.

He was bent over at the time, looking at the tool work on the table, when suddenly, one, two . . . six objects whistled just over his head, struck the opposite wall, and clattered to the floor. Jay dropped to the floor by reflex, as did all the others.

"A snare," Dr. Cooper exclaimed.

Jay was staring transfixed at the six deadly arrows that had nearly killed him when Ben-Arba shouted, "The idol, Dr. Cooper!"

The hawk idol had come to life! Leaping out from the wall, it brandished the spear; its big yellow eyes glistened. A horned demon also stepped forward, and then a fierce beast with a wolf's head.

None of the idols in the room were, in fact, idols. They were all very much alive, armed with deadly spears, and coming speedily toward them.

"Let's call it a day," Dr. Cooper ordered, and they all bolted for the same door by which they had entered.

The Wolf was near the door. He reached up with his spear and threw a lever on the wall.

There was a grinding sound and a creaking of pulleys, and a wooden crank next to the door began to spin in a blur as an immense slab of stone began to drop into the opening. The room would soon be sealed shut.

"Hurry!" Dr. Cooper yelled as the first spear whistled by his ear.

Ben-Arba dove under the sinking slab of stone, and then Dr. Cooper helped Lila through. Another spear just missed Jay as he scurried under the stone on his belly, his back actually brushing against the dropping slab.

Dr. Cooper slithered under the slab and made it

into the passageway as the stone came down like a deadly jaw, biting at his heels with a crushing thud.

They ran toward the entrance shaft, their light beams darting and sweeping, their frantic footsteps echoing up and down the passageway.

Ben-Arba cried out and came to an abrupt halt, the others nearly running into him.

The passage ended abruptly—they had come up against a solid wall!

"We've come the wrong way," Dr. Cooper concluded.

Ben-Arba could only shake his head. "I don't understand, Doctor!"

They turned and headed back the way they had come. Somewhere there had to be a passage they had missed. They found it, and just in time. They could hear the footsteps of their pursuers echoing up the tunnel behind them. They dashed down the passage, shining their lights everywhere, trying to spot that ventilation shaft. They ran for several yards but suddenly realized that nothing looked familiar. The carvings they had seen on the walls were not there, and neither were Jerry Frieden's flashlight, pick, and shoe.

"We've come the wrong way again!" Dr. Cooper moaned, not understanding.

Ben-Arba felt his legs hit a fine, invisible wire, but it was too late to stop.

"Ayyy, nooo!" he cried, falling in a heap.

Dr. Cooper skidded to the floor as if stealing a base as four more razor-sharp arrows zinged right over him and plinked off the opposite wall.

Ben-Arba was on his feet in a flash. "Hurry—we've sprung another snare!"

A huge stone plug fell from the ceiling, releasing a torrent of sand that began to rapidly fill the corridor. As the sand covered their feet, Lila wriggled and tumbled away from the deadly torrent. Jay fell as a crush-

ing stream of sand piled onto his back. Ben-Arba and
Dr. Cooper pulled at him and worked him free.

They ran down the corridor as it turned sharply to
the right, then sloped upward, then twisted down
again. Ben-Arba found a doorway in the left wall and
shined his light through it.

"This way, this way!" he shouted, frantically waving
his big gloved hand.

Dr. Cooper looked through the door and saw a
winding, stone stairway leading upward.

"Watch for snares," he cautioned Jay and Lila as he
hurried them through.

"Run, run!" shouted Ben-Arba.

The Coopers frantically ran up the stairs. The passageway was still rumbling and groaning behind them,
and they didn't know what would happen next.

Up, up the stairway went, winding this way and
that, a very large and dark passage through solid rock.
The steps were oversized, difficult, and steep.

They could see light filtering down from above
them, a dull orange glow. It had to be a way out.

Dust fell on their heads from above. Had they
sprung another trap? They bounded up the steps two
at a time, ducking under the low-hanging rocks, feeling
the stones quiver under their feet. The light above was
brighter with each step. It seemed to be the glow from
a fire.

Then they could see a doorway at the top of the
stairs and a firelit room just beyond it.

They reached the doorway and dove through it,
tumbling into the cavernous room just as a cloud of
dust burst upon them from the passage and a large
stone barricade fell across the doorway with thunderous impact.

"Mr. Ben-Arba!" Jay cried, "He's still in there!"

There wasn't time to think about it. They were all
struck motionless.

They had fallen right at the feet of the Hawk, the horned demon, and the Wolf. Hideous, living idols stood all around them, and the points of a dozen deadly spears were right under their noses.

Nearby, a familiar bonfire crackled and flickered. They were back in the ceremonial room, the very room they had fled from.

And they were surrounded.

# FOUR

One towering figure, a strange being with a fanged, bulb-eyed, horned, devilish mask and a long, crimson cloak, took a step toward them, then stopped rather casually, arms crossed, studying them.

The other figures were frightening in appearance, and looked ready to use their spears if the Coopers made one false move. In addition to the deadly spears, each carried a long, glimmering sword at his waist. Three were images of birds: the Hawk, an eagle, and what appeared to be a vulture. Three others were dressed like wild beasts: a lion, a wolf, and a monstrous, savage animal beyond description. Three, besides the one in the crimson cloak, wore frightening, demonic masks. And the last three looked like creatures that weren't of this earth at all. The Coopers were tightly surrounded by this fearsome, unflinching, silent dozen, and all around that circle, eleven deadly spears were lowered, the razor-sharp points aimed and very convincing.

Dr. Cooper and the crimson-cloaked figure exchanged long, steady stares as they sized up each other. The crimson figure just stood there for the longest time, not moving, arms crossed, as if waiting for something.

"Well," Dr. Cooper said softly, "I would say they have the upper hand."

The crimson man seemed to understand Dr. Cooper's words. He extended his hand toward Dr. Cooper, palm up. Dr. Cooper understood that, and handed over his gun.

The crimson figure nodded. That was what he was waiting for. He took some steps toward them, pointing across the cave. They looked where he was pointing and could see a cave entrance-exit that had not been there before. The other figures began prodding and leading them toward the entrance as the crimson leader followed. Not one of these strange beings said a word.

"The Yahrim?" Lila whispered.

"Their holy men, apparently," said Dr. Cooper, "and I'm afraid we stumbled into the middle of a religious ceremony."

"The Yahrim," Jay muttered. "The Fearful. They don't look too fearful to me. They don't look afraid of anything."

"Well," said Lila, *"they're* pretty scary."

Dr. Cooper explained in a hushed voice, "Their costumes evidently portray different qualities of their god: fierceness, cunning, bravery, terror, those sorts of things. Just keep praying that the Lord will bring some answers out of this."

"I'll be happy if He just brings *us* out of this," said Jay.

"Amen to that," said Lila.

They passed through the cave's low entrance and out into the warm, starry night, following a trail through the rocky terrain. The Coopers' beastly escorts were quite skilled in their work—they left no gaps for escape, and their spears were always just one wrong move away from the Coopers' ribs.

They followed the trail up a hill, then down into a rocky ravine, its cliffs on either side washed a deathly white by the silver light of the moon. At the end of the ravine, a steep path climbed up among the cliffs, and then, almost as a reminder that the Coopers were still on Planet Earth, the sound of goats and sheep met their ears. They were approaching a village.

When they reached the top of the cliffs, they saw a very steep hillside just beyond, a hillside dotted with many small windows glowing with the orange light of lanterns. As they came nearer, the Coopers were amazed to find that the windows were in houses built right in the hillside itself. The homes had been carved and chiseled out of the limestone side by side, one atop the other, all the way up the hill, stacked like a complex of crude apartments.

"Well!" Dr. Cooper exclaimed. "Cliff dwellers! Look at the stonework! Incredible!"

They entered the village along the main thoroughfare, a rough and rock-strewn trail which immediately became a very steep path with switchbacks that wound between, around, and over the tops of many dwellings, steadily taking the Coopers and their captors higher and higher up the hill. The village smelled of sweat, woodsmoke, and filth. These people were impoverished, and their life was obviously hard and demanding. The Coopers were drawing stares from weary, weathered goatherds and ragged mothers with babies, from sheepskinned, barefoot children chewing on leathery wheatcakes, and from old, white-haired elders. To see twelve bizarrely costumed apparitions walking by with spears and swords didn't seem to bother these people at all—seeing three fair-skinned strangers in western clothing *did*.

One little man stopped short and looked at them with his eyes wide and his mouth dropping open. It was the one-legged goatherd they'd already met in the hills above the dig. They tried waving a greeting, but he would not look them in the eye and quickly put on a face that said he'd never seen them before.

They climbed and climbed, and finally reached the top of the hill and the highest dwelling of all, a rather large, skillfully carved cavern with several windows, an impressive, torchlit entrance, and a broad, flat ledge in front that afforded a sweeping view of the entire village.

They approached the entrance, and for the first time a gap in the circle of guards opened, allowing the Coopers to follow the crimson figure to the big wooden door.

The crimson leader called out a command, and every man suddenly dropped to his knees with his face to the ground, moaning a chant of worship. As if in response, the big door opened, and a little, gray-haired man in a black robe bowed and beckoned. The crimson figure waved at the Coopers to follow him inside. They walked slowly through that door, not at all comfortable about it, feeling they could be walking into a deadly trap. The Hawk and the Wolf came in behind them, still brandishing their spears.

The little, gray-haired man closed the door behind them and then stood there to guard it. There were at least a dozen other guards already inside, armed with spears and swords, eyeing the prisoners suspiciously.

The Coopers surveyed the room and were startled at how beautiful it was in comparison to the poverty they had seen in the village below. It was a man-made cave, a roomy apartment carved out of stone, illuminated by several oil lamps and a pleasant, crackling fire in a large fireplace. The wood furniture was ornately carved and even studded with jewels. Goat and sheepskins covered the floor; colorful tapestries and handcrafts adorned the walls. This had to be the home of the tribal chief, the fabulously wealthy lord of these bizarre people.

The crimson figure reached up and carefully removed his mask. He was a tall, strong, and handsome man, his face wet with sweat, his brow furrowed with silent anger as he looked at the Coopers for just a moment. Then, with a gesture toward the back of the room, he finally spoke in broken English. "All you, wait there."

With that, he turned quickly and left the room through a low doorway.

Encouraged by a rude nudge from some guards, Dr. Cooper, Jay, and Lila went quickly to the back of the room and stood there against the wall. Another man was there already, one of the Yahrim, small in stature, very ragged, and trembling with fear. The Coopers all looked at each other, and then at the Hawk and the Wolf, still wearing their masks, still pointing those spears. None of them thought that talking would be a good idea at this point, but all their faces said the same thing: "What now?"

They heard the Man in Crimson returning. He reentered the room through the low doorway and then stood beside it at attention, obviously giving reverence to whoever would come through it next.

The little Yahrim man beside the Coopers gasped as a woman appeared. She was elderly and silver-haired but still beautiful, with very fair skin, dressed in fine silks and furs, her hands tucked together inside a snow-white fleece. Gold jewelry sparkled on her arms, her neck, and her waist, and her blue eyes were alert and cunning. She didn't look like she belonged in this place, among these people. She was clearly not one of them.

The Man in Crimson announced her in the Yahrim language and then in English as he glared at the Coopers, his eyes full of resentment. "The Ruler of the Yahrim and High Priestess of Ha-Raphah, Mara the Sorceress!"

At the crimson man's announcement, every man in the room dropped to his knees again and paid homage. The Coopers remained on their feet, and that brought a cold and angry stare from the Sorceress.

Dr. Cooper removed his hat and tried to be polite. "Hello."

The woman spoke in clear English, but her words

came slowly, hissing with anger. "American, you do not bow before Mara the Sorceress?"

"We bow only before the one true God and His Son, Jesus Christ."

"Christians . . ." she muttered to herself, and then spat in hatred. She barked a command to the others, and they all jumped to their feet.

She studied the Coopers for another long moment, then let her gaze fall upon the little Yahrim man standing beside them. She seemed even more angry at him—if that was possible—and gave the guards some orders. Responding immediately to her command, the guards grabbed the man and dragged him forward, forcing him to his knees in front of Mara as she took her seat in a very regal-looking, fur-lined chair in the corner.

The man began to whimper in fear. The Sorceress first glared at him with cold and ruthless eyes and then shouted questions at him.

Dr. Cooper listened intently. He whispered to his children, "It's a very corrupt dialect of Aramaic. I can hardly make it out, but . . . apparently this man owes the woman some taxes of some sort . . ."

The little man whimpered and seemed to be trying to explain.

"He's begging for more time," said Dr. Cooper. "Something about his crops failing . . . a goat dying . . ."

The Sorceress laughed at the man before replying to his words.

Dr. Cooper leaned and whispered in disbelief, "She . . . demands payment of the tax . . . She is offering him a terrible choice . . ."

The woman leaned forward and spat her words at the man.

Dr. Cooper was shocked. "She says he can pay double the tax immediately . . . or surrender his oldest daughter to her . . . to be her slave!"

The man fell on his face before the woman, crying and pleading desperately on his daughter's behalf. But the Sorceress only nodded to the guards, who grabbed the man roughly and dragged him out. Then she barked an order to some other guards.

"She says, 'Bring me the girl,' " Dr. Cooper whispered.

Two guards left immediately to carry out Mara's order.

Now it was the Coopers' turn. The Sorceress looked at them with the same, cold stare and then nodded toward some soft, comfortable chairs facing her throne.

The Coopers moved slowly toward the chairs she had indicated, looking at the Hawk and the Wolf to make sure it was all right with them. It seemed to be. Dr. Cooper sat in the middle chair, directly facing Mara the Sorceress; Jay and Lila sat in the chairs on either side of him. The Man in Crimson took his place standing beside the lady's throne.

She looked them over for a moment, and then said rather coolly, "You have come at a very bad time for strangers. It is the time of sacrifice and worship of The Fearsome One, a most sacred time for our people. This will be the first, the last, and the only time you will receive a kind and hospitable reception from me. You will state your identity and your business here."

"I am Dr. Jacob Cooper, archaeologist from America, and these are my children, Jay and Lila. Our business here—"

"Why were you trespassing in the Tombs of the Anakim?" she demanded.

Dr. Cooper made a note of the name she'd mentioned, and then tried to give an answer. "That was certainly not our intention. We had to enter the tombs to find one of our men, whom we believe is in great danger! He ventured down a ventilation shaft and apparently had some kind of accident . . ."

"Accident!" The woman laughed maliciously. "Tell me—did you hear singing?"

Dr. Cooper exchanged glances with his children and then looked once again at the Sorceress. "Yes, our men did hear something."

She nodded a deep, slow nod, smiling with delight. "Ah . . . and did you ever find your missing worker?"

"No, we—"

"Nor shall you!" she snapped, her cold eyes even colder. "Your foolish little man now belongs to Anak Ha-Raphah, who has done to him as he wishes—just as he will do to you if you remain here."

Dr. Cooper slowly leaned forward in his chair. Jay and Lila could tell the wheels were turning very fiercely in his head. "You said . . . Anak. The Fearsome One's name is *Anak?*"

The lady's face crinkled with a sly smile. "You have heard the name?"

"We have a holy book in which he is mentioned, along with his descendants, and there is a saying, 'Who can stand—' "

" '—before the sons of Anak!' " she interrupted. "You speak of the Hebrew Scriptures, yes?"

"Yes, the Old Testament, the words of Moses and the prophets."

"Then you know of the sons of Anak, the Anakim, and their might, their power, their fierceness."

"And the tombs were carved by *them?*"

"Of course. And now the tombs belong to Anak Ha-Raphah himself, and we are the Yahrim, who fear Anak as one fears death and who worship him in his tombs. He is our fearsome god."

"Then we must apologize for intruding. I assure you we meant no harm."

She only sneered at him. "You have done us no lasting harm, Jacob Cooper, except to interrupt our worship." She smiled a witchy smile. "And to trigger some of Anak's little surprises."

Dr. Cooper understood. "You're referring to the snares we encountered in the tombs? The tripwires, the hidden arrows, the falling sand?"

The Sorceress laughed in delight. "The handiwork of Ha-Raphah. He is insanely jealous for his tombs and his treasures. Many others have tried to dig in that valley, searching for Anak's treasures, and we have watched as Anak took care of them all, by snare, by stealth, by terror, by the keen edge of his horrible sword. Your man is dead, I assure you. Withdraw, and no one else will die. Consider the loss of one man a just payment for your intrusion."

Dr. Cooper spoke with great regret. "It might be *two* men now. Another was lost just before we were captured by your holy men."

Mara the Sorceress shook her head in disgust. "All for Anak's treasure, Doctor? What wealth could be worth your men's lives?"

Dr. Cooper spoke clearly and carefully. "It was not our purpose to find any treasure."

"My necklace!" she called to the Man in Crimson, who immediately reached into an ornate, wooden chest beside Mara's throne and brought out a dazzling, brilliant necklace of diamonds and emeralds. He very carefully, very reverently placed the piece around her neck, then bowed to her as he backed away.

Mara the Sorceress sat there for a moment, letting Dr. Cooper have a good look at her fabulous jewels.

"These do not tempt you, Doctor? You did not come here to steal wealth such as this?"

Dr. Cooper was not impressed with all that glitter. "No. The jewels are yours. I only came for what knowledge I could gain."

"*Knowledge,* Doctor?" she asked. She obviously considered him a liar. "You are a lover of *knowledge?*"

She cried out an order to the Hawk and the Wolf.

Sudden terror filled the room like an explosion. With stony indifference and one deadly move, the

Hawk grabbed Jay by his hair and held him in his chair with an iron grip. Just as quickly, the Wolf did the same to Lila. Neither child could move or escape their strength.

Then, with a droning, metallic ring, the Hawk and the Wolf each drew out a glimmering, razor-sharp sword and brought the edge right up to each child's throat.

Dr. Cooper knew it would be certain death for his children if he moved a muscle. He sat very still, not stirring, trying to give Jay and Lila courage with his eyes. More importantly, he was praying, and he knew they were. The Sorceress remained in her chair, smiling a wicked smile, the lives of the two children in her hands.

Then the Sorceress spoke slowly and cruelly. "A little game, Doctor, for the lives of your children? If you are truly a lover of knowledge . . ." She laughed mockingly. "We shall see, Doctor. We shall see."

# FIVE

Dr. Cooper remained motionless. He could tell the Sorceress was baiting him, testing him in a war of nerves. He kept an eye on Jay and Lila. Brave kids, they sat very still.

Mara waited for just a few moments to let the terror fully sink in, and then spoke.

"What kind of man are you really, Dr. Cooper?" she asked with a malicious mocking. "One who truly loves knowledge above riches? We will see . . . we will see." She looked at Jay, still in the Hawk's clutches, and smiled wickedly. She leaned forward and gazed at Dr. Cooper as she said, "For the life of your son, Doctor, answer me this riddle: 'It fills the heart, but craving still, man, though full, it cannot fill.' "

Dr. Cooper knew Jay was praying, and he prayed himself, even while he returned the evil gaze of the Sorceress. The answer came to him.

"Greed," he said. "It fills the heart of man, and man, even though filled with riches, is never satisfied."

The woman raised one eyebrow, and then nodded to the Hawk. The Hawk released Jay, and Jay tried breathing—a privilege he was very thankful to have again. Dr. Cooper offered a silent prayer of thanks.

"Very good, Doctor," said Mara. "And now, for the life of your daughter: 'It crushes the weak, it rules the poor; but he who owns it, it rules the more.' "

Lila was very, very still, waiting and praying, her face getting paler with each passing second. Dr. Cooper prayed too, looking at the edge of that sword only a fraction of an inch from Lila's neck.

*Thank you, Lord,* Dr. Cooper prayed silently. He had the answer for this riddle as well. "Power crushes the weak and rules over the poor, but he who owns it is enslaved by it; it rules him most of all."

The woman's eyes grew wide. She was impressed. She nodded to the Wolf, and he released Lila. Both Dr. Cooper and Lila breathed a loud sigh of relief.

"You *are* a lover of knowledge, Doctor," she said. "A man of great wit . . ."

Dr. Cooper was watching the situation carefully, and he noticed the faint nod of the woman's head and the shadow of the Wolf falling across his chair. The Wolf's powerful arm took hold of Dr. Cooper's head as the beast's sword came at his throat, but Dr. Cooper's legs flipped up in a flash and clamped around the Wolf's neck. In an instant, the Wolf sailed over the chair and Dr. Cooper and landed on his back with a thud. The wolf mask went sailing end over end through the air, and now the Wolf was just a sheepish, embarrassed man, his sword suddenly in Dr. Cooper's hand.

Dr. Cooper stood ready, holding the sword, his eyes on everyone in the room. The Sorceress watched in amazement.

She kept watching, apparently waiting for something.

"Well?" she finally asked. "He is yours! Do to him as you wish!"

"That will be quite enough!" Dr. Cooper scolded, his patience at an end. "We've had enough of your games and your riddles, and there will certainly be no bloodshed!"

She only leaned back and looked at him with awe.

"A rare kind of man you are, Doctor, a very special man."

"A man who wants no trouble and means no harm."

She leaned forward and asked intently, "And has not come to take Anak's treasure?"

Dr. Cooper leaned forward a little himself. "No, I have not!"

She studied him for a moment and then said, "If you are here for any other reason, you are indeed the first." Then she smiled a crafty smile and said, "You have tested very well, Doctor. I find you to have great prowess, and also a strong spirit to rule and contain it." She suddenly lowered her voice as if she wanted no one else to hear. "Could it be that you are a man worthy to challenge Anak?"

"Challenge *what?* What is this Anak? All you've given me is your superstitious talk about your god, your pagan religion, your tricks, and your riddles. But I still have one man possibly dead and another trapped in those tombs of yours, and I don't need any more idle talk about ghosts, spirits, or so-called gods!" Dr. Cooper calmed himself and said more quietly, "My concern is for my two lost men. All I want to do is find them, if they're still alive. Please, I need facts, concrete answers."

"Something you can see with your eyes, Doctor?" She removed both her hands from under the fleece where she'd kept them all this time.

The Wolf, Hawk, and Man in Crimson turned away in horror and started humming *The Song of Ha-Raphah.* Dr. Cooper was struck silent. Jay looked on in horror. Lila felt sick.

The woman held both hands in front of her, palms forward, fingers spread.

Dr. Cooper looked twice. Jay even counted.

Each hand had not five, but *six* fingers.

The woman's voice dropped to a low, ominous tone. "You have seen it, Doctor, with your own eyes: the Sixth Finger of the Anakim, the badge of ultimate power! These others have learned to fear it, as will you, for you will find that Anak *is* the Fearsome One, as real as these hands."

Dr. Cooper was stunned, so much information was suddenly taking form in his mind. "The Anakim . . ." he said with great wonder. "In Second Samuel . . . a giant from Gath, a man with six fingers on each hand, six toes on each foot."

"And of all the giants, of all the fearsome ones, not one was mightier or more fearsome than Anak, and it is his spirit that rules over the Tombs of the Anakim and over his people, the Yahrim. And I, Mara, am his High Priestess, appointed by Ha-Raphah himself, for only a true descendant of Anak can rule as priest."

"A direct descendant . . . of the Anakim!" said Dr. Cooper in awe.

"As such, my power and rule over the Yahrim is limitless. Ha-Raphah says it is to be, and it is so."

"And if anyone should oppose you?"

"They must face Anak, of course."

"And to paraphrase the saying, 'Who can stand before Anak?' "

Mara the Sorceress smiled a cunning smile and said, "Now do you have your facts, Doctor?"

She tucked her hands inside the fleece again and told her aides she had done so. The Hawk, Wolf, and Man in Crimson turned toward her again.

"You will be released," she said to the Coopers, "but you should know that you have trespassed—and on a sacred night of sacrifice for us. Be assured, anyone who disturbs Anak at such a time always pays a horrible price. If you are faint of heart, and if you fear death, you must forsake your quest here and leave the tombs immediately."

"And my two men?"

"Dismiss any thought of them." Leaning forward in her chair, she almost seemed to challenge Dr. Cooper by saying, "Consider them dead." She waited to hear his reply.

Dr. Cooper pondered her words for a moment. As Jay and Lila watched him, they knew what he was going to say. "Where can I find Anak?"

That answer seemed to be the one she expected. She shook her head in pity, but her eyes were smiling. "You are not that mighty . . ."

"My *God* is mighty."

Now her eyes became cold and penetrating as though she was trying to stare Dr. Cooper down. "Mightier than *my* god, Jacob Cooper? You speak as a foolish man, one who has never seen the stars blotted out by Anak's form, who has never stood in Anak's shadow and known his life will end horribly in that very instant. You will never find Anak, Doctor; *he* will find *you*. His spirit is everywhere . . . silent, cunning, more vicious than you can possibly imagine. He watches us all, but is never seen; he kills, and not a sound is heard. We always know where he has been, but never where he will be."

Dr. Cooper remained unshaken. "Where can I find him?"

The archaeologist's determined courage impressed the Sorceress. She looked into his eyes for a moment, studying him, pondering his words. She looked him up and down, considering his strengths.

"If your God is so mighty," she said, "and you put such great trust in Him . . . let the two of you discern these words." Then, with a wry and mocking smile, she began to sing *The Song of Ha-Raphah,* singing actual lyrics to the melody in a strange language.

Dr. Cooper listened intently until she finished, and then asked, "A riddle?"

She smiled wickedly. "You know not the answer?"

Dr. Cooper thought for a moment, then shook his head. "Perhaps because I'm not playing for the lives of my children."

With a very wily glint in her eyes, the Sorceress replied, "Oh, but you will be, Jacob Cooper. *You will be.*" Dr. Cooper was about to ask her what she meant, but she abruptly said, "Our visit is over. You are released."

The Hawk and the Wolf—minus his frightening mask—escorted the Coopers from the Sorceress' cave and back the way they had come. Dr. Cooper immediately took out his writing pad and scribbled down the strange words to the song the Sorceress had sung. So far they were meaningless, and even though he tried asking the Hawk and the Wolf about the song and its words, the two gruesome escorts remained stubbornly silent and mysterious.

Their path took an unexpected twist and did not return to the ceremonial cave where the Coopers had first been captured. Rather, the Hawk and the Wolf led them over a hill, through a dry riverbed, and then up a very steep trail to the brow of another hill, where they stopped. It was only now that the Coopers knew where they were: they could see their camp in the valley below, a tiny little cluster of tents pitched next to the unearthed Philistine temple of Dagon. Bill and Jeff were there by the fire, rifles in their hands, wary and tense.

The Hawk handed Dr. Cooper's gun back to him, and then he and the Wolf were gone, their mission accomplished. The Coopers hurried down the hill to the camp.

Dr. Cooper saw Bill raise his rifle. "Bill! It's us!"

The stunned look on the two men's faces was almost comical, and there was a significant time lapse before they broke into ecstatic smiles and started hollering, "Doc! Jay and Lila! Well, praise the Lord!"

Then came the reunion, the laughter, the hugs.

"We thought we'd lost you for sure!" Bill said with tears in his eyes.

"We didn't know *what* to do!" Jeff added.

"Well," said Dr. Cooper, "we have a lot to fill you in on. But what about Talmai Ben-Arba? Has there been any sign of him?"

"Nothing," said Jeff.

"Oh, great!" muttered Bill. "So now we've lost him too, huh?"

"I don't know. That big guy is so wily, there's no telling *what* happened to him."

"So what happened to *you?*" asked Bill.

The Coopers all looked at each other, sharing an incredible story they couldn't wait to tell.

"Well, let's talk about it over some food," said Dr. Cooper.

They gathered around the campfire as Bill opened some rations.

"We need some firewood," Lila observed.

"Fine," said Dr. Cooper. "Don't go too far."

"Okay."

She went toward the hills to see what she could find.

Dr. Cooper bit into a cold, leftover biscuit and related their experience with the Yahrim holy men and the very mysterious Mara the Sorceress. Bill and Jeff were amazed. Jay cringed a little just in remembering it.

Then a pressing question came to Jay's mind. "Dad, that riddle game she played with you . . . Just what was that all about?"

Dr. Cooper drew a deep breath. He could still feel the tension of that moment, and he was so glad it was over. "It revealed a definite Philistine influence on the Yahrim culture. Even Samson was involved in that sort of thing in the Book of Judges—the old Philistine custom of bantering and challenging with riddles."

"Well, I didn't appreciate that game at all. What if you had answered wrong?"

Dr. Cooper only shook his head. "Well, praise God for His grace. If I hadn't been so upset about Mr. Pippen's *greed,* and Mr. Andrews' obsession with *power,* I may not have had the right answers on my mind. But Mara had to have a reason for all those games. It was like she was testing me, not only in knowledge, but in physical prowess. First there was the riddle game, and then the mortal challenge from that wolf character."

"I thought you did really well!" Jay said proudly.

"Well, so did she, apparently." With that, Dr. Cooper took out his writing pad and looked at the strange words to the song she'd sung. "But I don't think the game's over."

"What do you have there?" asked Bill.

"A song . . . a riddle . . . whatever. It's like she's almost *daring* us. As soon as she knew we wouldn't be leaving until we faced this Anak, whoever or whatever he is, she sang this song to me, and . . . if it's another Philistine riddle game, it has to be some kind of clue, a piece of vital information."

"Well done, Doctor!" came a very sudden and startling voice from the darkness beyond the camp.

Every weapon they had was immediately in hand and aimed toward that booming voice.

"Well . . ." said Talmai Ben-Arba, stepping into the light of the campfire, "again we meet, and again I receive the same heavily armed welcome!"

Dr. Cooper stood to his feet and pushed his hat back a little, an unconscious gesture that showed he was quite surprised and very, very curious.

There just wasn't that much free, dead, burnable wood in this kind of country. The short, scrubby brush was a very tough sort of plant, so intent on surviving that it wasn't about to leave any dead branches lying around. Lila found a few sticks here and there, but had just about resigned herself to returning to camp with far less than a full armload.

She looked back. Oh-oh. She'd gone around the hill now, out of sight of the camp, and she knew that wasn't safe. She decided to start back.

What was that? It sounded like a child crying. She stood very still and listened. There it was again, and it sounded very desperate.

She set the wood down near a large rock she'd be able to find again and headed toward the sound.

Ben-Arba looked none the worse for wear and answered the question at hand without Dr. Cooper having to ask it. "I escaped by another route, Doctor. The tombs have many available to the one who knows where to find them. And as for your thoughts on Mara the Sorceress and her cryptic riddles . . . Yes, you have her well figured out. Her words *do* have meaning, Doctor, for the man who can decipher them. You would be wise to always consider every word she says . . . Every *letter* of every word." He looked at the sky and said excitedly, "Ah, the moon is getting lower!"

Dr. Cooper couldn't care less about the moon. He looked at Ben-Arba for a long, long time before he said anything, then finally motioned the big man to a nearby stone. "Have a seat, Talmai. We have a few things to discuss."

Lila noticed it was suddenly getting darker and saw the moon sinking down behind the mountain. Now she was really torn between seeking out the crying she heard and hurrying back to camp. It was getting very dark and scary out here.

There it was again—a fearful cry, someone in trouble! She was getting very close now. She could hear it somewhere below her. Not far down the hillside was a deep ravine. It was coming from there.

She found a path that led down the hill. She would find out what it was and then get right back to camp. Her heart was starting to pound. She was beginning to feel she'd been away from camp far too long.


Dr. Cooper and Ben-Arba sat by the small, smoldering fire nose to nose, and Dr. Cooper had all the sternness he needed to outweigh Ben-Arba's stubbornness.

"Keep going," Dr. Cooper said. "I want you to tell me just how much you know about this Sorceress lady."

But Ben-Arba kept looking toward the horizon. "Soon the moon will set behind that mountain. It will be Ha-Raphah's moment."

"Just answer my question!" Even Dr. Cooper's patience was wearing thin.

Ben-Arba gave a disgusted sigh and grudgingly answered, "What you said about the riddle caught my attention. The words of Mara the Sorceress always mean more than you think. The answers to the riddles, for instance: greed and power."

"She chose those riddles for a reason?"

Ben-Arba looked at the moon again. "It won't be long."


Lila reached the edge of the ravine, and the beam of her flashlight caught a small white creature.

"A baby goat!" she said, immediately filled with pity.

The little goat was caught in a pit in the rocks. Bleating, it paced back and forth, trying to find a way out.

Lila looked for a way to reach it, found a likely route down, and then called, "Hang on, little fella! I'm coming!"


Ben-Arba had the moon, and only the moon, on his mind. "Doctor, have I told you enough? May we move on to what else I know?"

"All right, all right. What's this you keep saying about the moon?"

Ben-Arba grabbed his rifle, an excited glimmer in his eye. "Tonight is the night of sacrifice, Doctor! During the nights of the full moon, the Yahrim leave a sacrifice for Ha-Raphah. Whatever is left for him, be it a sheep or a goat or bags of grain, it is gone without a trace when morning comes. *Something* consumes it. If we hurry, we may be able to see what it is!"

Dr. Cooper and the others couldn't believe what they'd heard. They sprang to their feet.

"You could have told me this before!" said Dr. Cooper.

"Ehhhh, I tried, I tried," Ben-Arba insisted.

Then a thought hit them all. "Where's Lila?"

Ben-Arba grabbed Dr. Cooper's arm. "Lila—the girl? She is not here?"

"No, she—"

Ben-Arba's expression changed from one of excitement and glee to one of incredible horror. "She is . . . out there?"


With careful steps and just the right handholds, Lila lowered herself into the pit. The little goat hurried over to her and nuzzled her leg.

"Hey, it's okay, little guy—I'm here."

She gave the goat a pet and a scratch, and then . . .

A flute began to play.

Lila withdrew her hand from the goat as if she'd been burned. She listened. The flute sounded far away, but she could hear the melody clearly.

*The Song of Ha-Raphah.*

Dr. Cooper, Jay, Bill, and Jeff were ready, armed like a small army, and so was Ben-Arba. They stormed from the camp, following Ben-Arba's leading.

"How far?" Dr. Cooper asked.

"It depends on where it is," said Ben-Arba. "There are many pits and crevices in the rocks where the sacrifices are left. We must find the one they have chosen to use this night."

"Lila!" they called, but no answer came.

Ben-Arba stopped short. "No . . ."

They could all hear it. Other voices were joining now, singing and wailing that eerie melody.

"They are calling to him!" said Ben-Arba. "Don't make a sound, please! It is death to trespass upon the site of a sacrifice. You will bring their spears down on us!"

Dr. Cooper listened carefully. "The singing seems to be centered around that ravine down there."

"Yes, that is one of the places for sacrificing," said Ben-Arba.

They headed for it, moving toward the singing, feeling like they were walking into a black and threatening storm.

Lila was scared. *The Song of Ha-Raphah* was swirling and echoing all around her in that rocky pit, droning in her ears, making her shiver. She picked up the little goat.

"C'mon, let's get out of here!"

With careful but hurried steps, she began to climb

out of the pit. One step, then another, a handhold here, a handhold there. She wondered if she could possibly get out in time.

She gasped and thought her heart would stop. Just above her head, a gruesome, grinning, demonic face, an eerie mask hanging on a wooden stake, leered down at her. Now she was more than scared.

Dr. Cooper and the others found a small bundle of firewood. Beyond that was a likely path toward the ravine. Ben-Arba threw the bolt on his rifle, ramming a cartridge into the chamber. The others did the same, then hurried down the path.

Lila was anxiously looking for the path out of the ravine. The moon was gone now, and the darkness hid everything. She pressed ahead, shining her light this way, then that way. The goat was fidgeting in her arms.

"What's the matter, boy?" she asked.

Behind her, a star close to the horizon vanished. Then a star just above it disappeared as well. There was absolutely no sound.

But Lila could feel a *presence*. She kept looking for the path. She thought she found it and headed for it.

More stars disappeared, higher and higher in the sky. A shadow began to form, an area where no stars could be seen. It grew ominously, rising steadily out of the earth.

Lila finally, gratefully found the path. She quickened her step. The little goat began to whimper.

Ben-Arba led the others to the edge of the ravine. He saw something there. With an anguished and muffled cry he bounded down the hillside.

The others were startled.

"What is it?" Bill asked.

Jay saw it first and couldn't speak a word. He could only grab his father and point frantically.

Dr. Cooper saw it and dashed down the hillside right behind Ben-Arba.

Lila kept struggling up the hill, trying to find the path through the rocks, the little goat wriggling and bleating in her arms. She could no longer hold the terrified animal.

"Okay, you can make it from here," she said, setting him on the ground.

The little goat dashed up the hill as if fleeing for its life.

Lila knew she was very, very frightened, but she realized she had to keep cool. She hurried up the path, trying not to panic.

Behind her, and without a sound, an immense, black pillar jutted into the sky like a thunderhead. It was shaped like a man, it had eyes, and it was moving toward her.

# SIX

Talmai Ben-Arba and Dr. Cooper stopped short on a precarious rock formation. They saw Lila far below, scrambling up the rocks, fleeing for her life. They could see a huge, black, hideous thing right behind her, a deep, man-shaped shadow swallowing up the starlight, hiding the ground beneath it.

Ben-Arba jerked his rifle to his shoulder.

"Anaaaaaaak!" he shouted as the rifle fired, the blue flame from the barrel lighting up the rocks.

They heard Lila scream. Dr. Cooper was on his way to her, with Jay, Jeff, and Bill right behind. The little goat went running by them in overwhelming terror. They could see Lila on the ground but could no longer see the shadow.

"Cover us!" Dr. Cooper ordered, and Jeff and Bill remained above, rifles ready, as he and Jay scrambled down the rocks.

All around them, *The Song of Ha-Raphah* melted into a horrible clammer of wails, like the cries of countless souls falling into hell.

Ben-Arba remained on the high rock pinnacle, his rifle ready, his eyes peering into the darkness, attempting to examine every shadow, every crevice between the rocks, every dark area on the landscape below that could possibly be his target. He didn't know if he'd hit it. He could see nothing.

A spear whistled by his ear. He spun and fired the

rifle at a small moving shadow. Another spear glanced off a rock just behind him. The Yahrim were attacking!

When Dr. Cooper and Jay got to Lila, she threw her arms around her father and held him, not saying a word, not crying, only gasping for air. He didn't hesitate a moment but carried her back up the trail.

The eerie, warlike cries of the Yahrim surged like angry waves all around them. Dr. Cooper hurried up the trail, ducking spears and arrows as he carried Lila. Jay watched behind them, and Jeff and Bill were above, still looking in every direction, trying to pinpoint the source of the deadly weapons.

The Yahrim, unseen in the darkness, were clambering down the rocks, moving in on them like a rockslide.

Ben-Arba searched for cover even while he looked for targets. "Savages! Fanatics!" he yelled at them, along with many filthy names in several different languages. He fired his rifle this direction, then that, in front, behind, spinning and looking about. But the arrows were coming out of the dark, and he couldn't see who was shooting them.

The Coopers ran by, and he followed them, firing several more shots at nothing in particular.

"Suddenly they're not so timid," Dr. Cooper called to him.

"Not when their god is with them!" said Ben-Arba.

"Did you see where it went?"

"It vanished, Doctor, and let us do the same!"

They fled back to camp, out from under that deadly shower of spears and arrows. The attackers did not follow them.

As for the ghost, the thing, the horrible god called Anak Ha-Raphah, it was gone. Just like that.


There was no peace in the camp that night. All around them, the hills were crawling with Yahrim, all unseen in the darkness, still calling to Ha-Raphah, still wailing and crying, hooting and howling, swishing through the stiff grass and clambering over the rocks. The night was black, and the air was alive with terror. Everything—the hills, the crazy people hiding in them, the cries and wails of those people, the ghost himself— seemed terribly close, terribly dangerous, like an avalanche of evil about to crush them all.

Ben-Arba, Bill, and Jeff, all heavily armed, were keeping watch around the camp. Dr. Cooper, Jay, and Lila were inside their tent, huddled around a lantern. Lila hadn't said a word since they'd found her on the ground back in the ravine. She was still shaking, staring, trying to find some words, but unable to. Jay and Dr. Cooper just held her close and prayed soothingly, hoping their prayers would also drown out the chilling sounds outside.

"I saw him, Dad," Lila said suddenly.

He hugged her. "I know."

"I saw him," she repeated simply because she had to. "I saw him."

"We did too," said Jay.

"He was there. He was looking right at me."

Dr. Cooper had plenty of questions, but he knew he had to wait. She had to be ready.

"Did you see how tall he was, Dad?"

Dr. Cooper didn't want to answer.

"Did you see how tall he was?" she asked again.

"I'm not sure," Dr. Cooper finally said. "It was hard to tell from where we were standing."

Lila was trying to think. "I've never seen anyone so big in my life . . ."

Dr. Cooper ventured a question. "Was it a *man*, Lila? Did it seem . . . human?"

She tried to think and tried to remember, but finally she could only shake her head. "I could only see his eyes. He was looking right at me, and . . ." She broke off her sentence and stared in silence for a moment. "He was going to kill me, wasn't he?"

"Shhhh . . ." Dr. Cooper said, holding her close. "It's over. You're safe now."

But she could hear the wailing of the Yahrim through the cloth walls of the tent. All three of them could. They did not feel safe.

They did not feel safe all night.

It wasn't a long night. Most of it had already been spent, and the sun was soon rising over the valley. Sometime before the light came, the Yahrim seemed to melt into the rocky terrain and their cries faded away. And as the darkness gave way to daylight, some of the horror went away with it. Bill and Jeff could see clearly now, which made them feel much more secure. Ben-Arba even lay down to catch a few winks of sleep.

Dr. Cooper emerged from the tent while the morning sky was still pink and the air still had the leftover chill of the night. He was tired, but his walk was firm and his eyes were determined. He joined Bill and Jeff beside the crackling breakfast fire.

"Thanks for keeping watch."

"No problem, Doc," said Jeff. "Get any sleep?"

"Enough for now, I suppose. The kids have been sleeping for a few hours."

"How's Lila?" Bill asked.

"She'll be ready for another day of it, I imagine. How are you two holding up?"

"We took turns on the watch," Jeff explained. "We got some sleep, but not much."

Dr. Cooper noticed Ben-Arba curled up in the sand near the edge of the camp, his rifle still in his hands, snoring in a catnap.

Dr. Cooper turned his back on Ben-Arba, beckoned to Bill and Jeff, and spoke in a lowered voice. "I don't want any more guessing games with Mr. Ben-

Arba. Bill, I want you to take the jeep into Gath and check around. See what you can find out about this guy—where he really comes from, if he has any family around here, and how long he's been interested in this so-called treasure. That guy knows too much to be a newcomer. Somehow he's connected with this whole thing, and I mean *closely* connected. I want to know exactly how."

"Yeah," said Bill, "I think it's about time. I'll go this morning."

"I'll be taking a walk with him before breakfast to check out that sacrificial site in the daylight. Take off after we're gone, and maybe he won't get curious."

There was a sleepy snort. Ben-Arba finally stirred and awoke from his restless sleep.

"Ehhh . . ." he muttered, looking around. "So that terrible night is over."

Dr. Cooper surveyed the surrounding hills. They were silent and empty now, just as before. It was as if the horrors of the night had never happened.

"Well, guys, how long before breakfast?" he said finally.

"Oh, I can get it started any time," said Jeff.

"Okay, give us another hour or so. In the meantime, Talmai, let's you and I take a hike."

Ben-Arba's bushy eyebrows arched. He grinned and picked up his rifle.

Bill picked up the keys to the jeep.


The trail back to the site of the sacrifice seemed much longer in the daylight. Perhaps this was because they weren't running for their lives in the dark. They made their way along very warily, watching for any movement in the rocks, listening for any sound. Nothing appeared, and all was deathly quiet. For all they knew, they were totally alone in this rocky, barren wasteland.

"Ah, a souvenir," said Ben-Arba, picking up an arrow from the sandy trail. The point was finely honed metal. He showed it to Dr. Cooper. "You could shave with this edge, Doctor."

Dr. Cooper needed no convincing. Ben-Arba kept the arrow, and they continued on their way.

Ben-Arba was feeling a little more conversational this morning. "You were right about the Philistine influence. At one time, the Yahrim were not called the Yahrim at all. They were originally a sect of the Philistines. They worshipped Dagon and all the other Philistine deities—that is, until Ha-Raphah came along."

"Last night you called him Anak," said Dr. Cooper.

Ben-Arba was caught off-guard, but then he smiled and laughed a little. "Well done, Doctor, well done! Yes, I know his name."

"What else do you know?"

Ben-Arba gave a shrug. "Maybe it *is* time to talk about it." He slung his rifle comfortably over his shoulder and began. "Anak appeared to these people about ten years ago, and it was then that they became the Yahrim, the Fearful Ones. Before that, they really had nothing to be afraid of. They had lived in these hills for generations as the last remaining Philistines, and they never gave any thought to the fact that this was originally the land of the Anakim, the fearsome giants. Why should they? The sons of Anak were gone, conquered by the invading Israelites under Joshua. Yes, there were a few scattered descendants like Goliath, who was killed by David. But those last remaining giants lived among the Philistines until they *became* Philistines, and that is the last anyone ever heard of the Anakim . . . until recently."

"When Anak himself appeared?"

"Anak's ghost, they say, returning to rule over the land taken from him so long ago. He was a horrible, terrifying, bloodthirsty spirit, demanding offerings, worship, and sacrifices!"

"And Mara the Sorceress?"

"She came into the village claiming to be his priestess. She rules over the Yahrim now, and they obey her out of sheer terror of Anak."

They could see the ravine where Lila had been and their own footprints leading hurriedly away from it. They made sure they had their weapons ready as they headed down.

They entered the ravine, where they found more arrows and some spears.

"For only a few hundred armed men, the Yahrim can rally quite an attack," Dr. Cooper observed.

"Mmm, but they still missed," said Ben-Arba.

Then they saw the rocky pit where the little goat had been. Now that it was day, the pit didn't look quite so dark and frightening, and the trail leading to it was easy to follow.

Ben-Arba stopped short. Dr. Cooper saw it too.

There, grinning in the sunlight, was a fiendish, demonic mask, mounted on a wooden stake and decorated with beads and feathers. It had a toothy, crooked smile on its face, and it was leering with huge, bulbous eyes into the pit.

Across the pit from this first gruesome spectator was another one, this time the bleached skull of a goat, mounted on another wooden stake, decorated with colorful ribbons that fluttered in the breeze. It too was staring into the pit.

There were other strange markers as well. As Dr. Cooper and Ben-Arba came to the pit's edge, they could count ten in all. There were other skulls of animals, more masks, some small religious carvings that looked like totem poles. Dr. Cooper noticed that several of them resembled the weird costumes the Yahrim holy men had been wearing in the ceremonial cave. All were facing into the pit.

Ben-Arba, looking carefully at each marker, explained, "These all had something to do with the sacrifice last night. This was a very sacred place."

Dr. Cooper looked carefully into the pit. It was not very deep, only about six feet, and about twenty feet across. The rock walls were steep, the sandy floor smooth and featureless.

"Well, this is where that thing came from," he said, finding a way to climb down.

Ben-Arba remained above, his rifle ready, as Dr. Cooper stepped down onto the sand. Dr. Cooper felt like he was standing in a small arena, with ten grisly spectators watching his every move. He looked all around the floor of the pit, but nothing caught his eye. There were no footprints other than Lila's and the goat's.

"Just what do you expect to find down there?" asked Ben-Arba.

"A clue, I guess. If that thing was real, it had to get in here somehow. It had to leave a mark or a print or *something.*"

Ben-Arba only shrugged. "Maybe yes, maybe no. A ghost lives by its own rules."

Dr. Cooper walked slowly around the pit, examining the rock walls. He saw no cracks or passages, no telltale seams.

He suddenly stopped—something didn't look quite normal. Toward the other end of the pit was a depression in the sand about the size of a dinner plate, but it was half-covered with what was certainly a fresh layer of sand, as if someone had tried to cover it up. He approached it carefully, testing each step he took.

What had made that little dip in the sand? What was—

The ground gave a little under his foot. He stepped back quickly, and the sand began to move.

Ben-Arba cocked his rifle. "What is it, Doctor?"

Dr. Cooper took a few more steps back, looking at that strange, moving sand.

It was as if a hole had suddenly opened under the sand. The sand was flowing downward toward a deep center, like grain down a funnel. The depression quickly grew wider and wider.

"Get back, Doctor, get back!" Ben-Arba shouted.

Dr. Cooper got clear of the sandy floor, perching on the rock wall of the pit as he continued to watch the sand disappear downward as if being consumed from beneath. Then, just as mysteriously as it had begun, the motion stopped, the sand came to rest, and the floor of the pit was smooth and flat once again.

"What was that, Doctor?" Ben-Arba asked, amazed.

Dr. Cooper was fascinated and very puzzled. He shook his head. "I . . . I haven't the slightest idea."

Just then there was a sound that pierced the desert silence: the bleat of a small goat. Ben-Arba looked up toward the hills and could see it.

"The sacrifice, Doctor," he said.

Dr. Cooper climbed out of the pit and could see the little goat bounding toward them over the rocks, its white coat shining brightly in the sunshine.

"Friendly little fellow, isn't he?" Dr. Cooper remarked.

The goat went first to Ben-Arba, who gave it a few scratches between its ears. Then Ben-Arba noticed the collar around its neck. He knelt to examine it.

"Mmm," he said. "Yes, this was the sacrifice, a gift from the old goatherd, One-Leg. This is his mark on the collar."

Dr. Cooper was very interested in that. "The goatherd missing a leg? We've met!"

Ben-Arba looked off toward the hills, voicing his thoughts as they came to him. "The goat is free and alive. Anak Ha-Raphah did not get his gift, thanks to our meddling last night. We have scorned his sacrifice, and someone will have to pay."

"What are you saying?"

Ben-Arba looked right at Dr. Cooper and said, "I

am saying the goatherd could be in grave danger, and it could be our doing."

The home of the little goatherd, One-Leg, was on the other side of the mountain from the cliff village of the Yahrim. Ben-Arba knew the way, and they all made the trip—none of them had any desire to be left alone. They hurried, hoping for the best, yet expecting the worst. The men carried their weapons and were ready for trouble. The little goat ran on ahead, eager to return home.

They came around the mountainside and finally caught sight of the humble stone and mud dwelling, perched on the side of the hill. Some goat pens were nearby. There was no sign of the goatherd.

Dr. Cooper instinctively crouched down, and the others did likewise. Something was definitely wrong.

"More of those markers," he said.

Jay and Lila got their first look at the strange, ceremonial markers of the Yahrim. All around the goatherd's little homestead were skulls, masks, hideous ornaments—all on brightly colored stakes, all facing inward toward the goatherd's dwelling, all decorated with ribbons, skins, feathers, weavings.

"They've been here, too," said Jeff.

Ben-Arba said slowly, "And I am afraid that *he* has also been here."

Ben-Arba's gaze toward the sky directed their attention to some huge, black vultures circling high overhead. Other scavengers were perched on the rocks above the goat pens. They were screeching in protest at being disturbed.

Dr. Cooper led the way, and the party slowly crept down the hill. The sun was hot, and the thick air carried some very unpleasant smells. The vultures screeched and fluttered up the hillside a few yards, and then a few more, and then a few more as these intruders kept coming closer. The masks on the stakes seemed to laugh at them with hideous, toothy expressions.

Soon they could see into the goat pen, and the sight wasn't pleasant.

The goats, about twenty of them, lay dead, thrown about the pen as if by a whirlwind. The little white goat bleated as it jumped through the broken fence and found its dead mother.

No one could say a word. They all stared at the sight until Dr. Cooper broke the spell of horror by moving on toward the house. They followed him, lagging just a little, their eyes darting everywhere.

Dr. Cooper rounded the corner of the home and stopped short, crouching, listening, his eyes wide. He beckoned to Ben-Arba and Jeff, who came closer with their rifles. Both men brought their rifles into readiness when they saw what Dr. Cooper saw.

The others came very slowly around the corner as well, and then froze a safe distance away.

There was no longer a doorway—an immense hole had been torn through the side of the house. The rough stones were strewn everywhere, and what used to be the door now lay here and there in splinters.

Dr. Cooper stepped forward, his gun ready in his hand, and ventured a look inside.

He instantly spun around and kept them all back with his hand.

"Jay, Lila," he said, his voice very controlled, "please step over there and wait for us."

He was gesturing to a small open area a little further around the house. They obeyed him and hurried toward it. When they were gone, Jeff and Ben-Arba stepped forward to join Dr. Cooper.

Ben-Arba took a look inside the house, and his face immediately twisted with horror and disgust. Jeff, shocked, slumped against the wall, taking deep breaths to recover.

Ben-Arba found a familiar wooden peg in the rubble and showed it to the others.

"One-Leg, the goatherd," Dr. Cooper said for all of them. "We're too late."

Jeff shook his head in horror and amazement. "I've hunted grizzlies and kodiaks and never seen any of them that could do *this.*"

Ben-Arba was strangely silent. Dr. Cooper saw a genuine fear in his face, a fear that had not been there before.

Ben-Arba could feel Dr. Cooper looking at him. He struggled for words. "He has grown much worse . . ." he whispered.

"What was that?" Dr. Cooper asked.

Ben-Arba seemed to be talking to himself as he muttered, "He has become a monster . . . Much worse . . . It was only a goat, only one little goat . . . There was no need to do this . . ."

A cry came just then from Jay and Lila—"Dad! Hey, everybody!"

The men dashed around the house in an instant, guns ready, expecting the worst.

Jay and Lila were all right—they'd found something on the ground. Dr. Cooper and the others hurried to see what it was.

"Ah!" said Ben-Arba.

Dr. Cooper sank to one knee, pushed his hat back a little, and nodded slowly to himself.

There before them, in one soft patch of ground, was the first direct evidence of whatever had been here: a footprint. Dr. Cooper held his forearm just above it, his elbow above the heel. His outstretched fingers fell short of the toes by a few inches. As for the toes, it was clear to see that they numbered six.

Dr. Cooper looked up at the others, particularly Ben-Arba. "Well, I guess it's good news and bad news."

He looked at the footprint again. "The good news is, a ghost doesn't leave tangible footprints. So now we know for sure this thing is physical, real, alive. The bad news is . . ." He looked back toward what was left of the goatherd's house.

"I think it's *all* bad news," said Jeff.

Ben-Arba was visibly shaken. The old cockiness was gone. "The news is *very* bad, Doctor. Never before has Anak Ha-Raphah shown such fierceness, such . . . rage. And never before has he ventured this far from the tombs to take a life."

"Take a life?" Lila asked fearfully.

Dr. Cooper put a gentle hand on her shoulder. "The old goatheard is dead. Murdered."

With merciless timing, an impatient vulture underlined Dr. Cooper's words with a rude screech.

Now Jay and Lila felt the same chilling sensation they could read in the faces of the others, that unshakable feeling that somewhere—up in the hills, among the rocks, hiding in the crevices, or maybe even closer than they dared to imagine—a monster was waiting, silently prowling, and they were all being watched, followed, *hunted*.

Lila could see the little goat still nuzzling its dead mother, and she struggled to ask, "I'm the one who ruined that sacrifice. Is it . . . is it my fault?"

Ben-Arba answered very firmly, "No, child. You did what was right, what any decent human would do. As for this beast, what difference could one little goat make? What we see here is the work of a demon, a monster. *He* is the one to blame!"

"And what about the Yahrim?" asked Jeff, looking around at all the gruesome markers. "Looks like they made a real party of it."

Dr. Cooper too was quite bothered about the markers. He looked at Ben-Arba. "Well, how about it? Do you have any idea what all these mean?"

Ben-Arba could feel Dr. Cooper's gaze cutting into

him. He finally answered, "I might," and looked carefully at the markers, one at a time, walking from one to the next. Sometimes he shook his head in puzzlement; at other times his eyes narrowed as if the marker was telling him something. Then he stood in the middle of them all and let his eyes move around the circle as if reading them.

He faced Dr. Cooper and said, "We should get back to our camp, Doctor, and very quickly."

# SEVEN

As soon as they could see the camp, Ben-Arba let out a growl of pain and anger and said, "I knew it."

Some new faces were waiting for them, twelve altogether, standing in a rough circle all around the camp, staring, laughing, mocking, as if guarding the area. Some were animal skulls; some were ugly, grinning masks; some were animal and bird carcasses.

Dr. Cooper didn't take another step closer to the camp until he'd had a good, long look at it. Everything seemed very quiet, and none of the tents or equipment had been disturbed.

Ben-Arba knew what everyone was wondering and finally said, "It should be safe. The Yahrim have done what they came for. They are gone."

They were all very cautious anyway, as they carefully chose each step into the valley. As they came near, they could see many recent footprints in the sand, and some were the clawed animal prints of the costumed Yahrim holy men.

The camp was intact. They checked the tents and the supply hut—nothing had been stolen or disturbed.

"So," Dr. Cooper concluded, "they came here for one purpose only—to surround our camp with these pagan markers." Dr. Cooper looked at Ben-Arba. "Talmai, the markers back at the home of One-Leg told you something. Can you tell us—and I mean tell us clearly—what these here might mean?"

Ben-Arba drew a deep breath and began walking around the circle of markers as he had done before, examining each one carefully. From the look on his face, the answer wouldn't be long in coming, and they probably would not like it.

Just then they all heard the roar of the jeep. Bill was just returning, kicking up a cloud of dust. He pulled to a stop just above the camp and waved at Dr. Cooper.

Dr. Cooper told Ben-Arba, "Keep working on it. I'll be right back."

With that, Dr. Cooper quickly went up to where Bill was waiting. As Ben-Arba kept eyeing and comparing the different markers, Dr. Cooper and Bill had a private conference.

Bill spoke in low, hurried words. "He's known, Doc, all over Gath. I'd even say he's famous. All I had to do was mention his name and I had people closing in on me, wanting to know what he was up to."

"So what is he up to?"

"Oh, he wants that treasure, all right, but he *is* closely connected with everything up here. Wait'll you hear *this* . . ."

Before long, Ben-Arba was ready with his explanation, and he began as soon as Dr. Cooper and Bill came down into the camp.

"This one," he said, pointing at a large mask with an ugly, white face, "is *you,* Dr. Cooper. This is the mask of the outsider, the invader, the unwelcome foreigner. And these here . . ."—Ben-Arba pointed to two images on either side of the white one—". . . are your children. This one with the golden hair is Lila, and this one, the symbol for the firstborn, is Jay. These two others are Mr. White and Mr. Brannigan."

Bill and Jeff looked at the horrible, ugly faces on the markers and sneered.

"Those Yahrim weren't too kind, were they?" said Bill.

"This one with the blank face symbolizes an unknown enemy. They probably mean me." Then Ben-Arba went to a very gruesome, pale mask with a horrified expression, splattered with red paint. "This one, I would guess, refers to the man you lost, your Jerry Frieden."

"What about all the others?" Dr. Cooper asked.

Ben-Arba scanned all the markers again, as if reading them. "They speak the same message as we saw at the sacrificial pit, and then at the home of One-Leg. These here, with the frightened expressions, speak of Ha-Raphah's great power and might. The dead birds and animals are a way of showing how cruel and ruthless he is, and how he spares no one. The skulls are symbols of death and destruction, and since they turn inward, toward us, they mean that death and destruction should also be turned toward us. It is the Yahrim's way of turning the anger of their god away from themselves and toward someone or something else."

"The whole idea of a sacrifice," said Dr. Cooper.

Ben-Arba nodded. "According to the markers back at the sacrificial pit, Anak Ha-Raphah is angry because strangers have trespassed in his tombs. The Yahrim feared he would vent his anger by coming after them—so they provided the goat for him to kill. That failed."

"Thanks to me," said Lila with regret.

"Anak and his followers blame the goatherd. They know he talked with you and your men, and they think it could have been a cowardly attempt to trap their god. Those markers at the home of One-Leg told of his horrible failure to please Anak by speaking to foreigners and letting them interfere with the sacrifice, and also told of all the horrible deaths he deserved to die until Anak was satisfied. Those markers were fulfilled, as we all saw. Since Anak could not kill the goat, he killed the owner of the goat."

"And now the markers surround *us,*" said Dr. Cooper.

Ben-Arba couldn't help feeling fear and despair as he went on, "Anak is much worse, much more of an animal now than he ever was. He is *still* angry. First the goat, then One-Leg. Next, the outsiders who trespassed . . ."

"The Yahrim are trying to sic Anak on *us!*" Jay concluded.

Ben-Arba looked again at all the markers, which seemed to surround them like ghastly guards. "The markers drew Anak to the goat . . . and then to the goatherd . . . And tonight, when the night is its darkest, they will draw him *here.* Anak Ha-Raphah will come for *us!*"

Ben-Arba's voice quivered just a little as he said it, and as he checked his gun again—even though it didn't need it—his hands trembled. He was trying to appear brave and powerful, but his fear was plain to see.

Dr. Cooper took a look at all the markers, then took several moments to scan the surrounding hills as he began to formulate a plan.

"Say, Bill," he said at last, "wasn't there a small settlement not too far down the road? I think they had some cattle there, some sheep, goats, livestock . . ."

"Yeah, that's right," Bill answered. "About five miles, I'd say. What are you thinking of?"

"Oh," said Dr. Cooper, looking toward the hills again, "I just thought it would be nice to have some straw."

"Straw?" asked Jeff.

"Yes. Two bales should do it."

Night fell like a slow, blackening curtain over the rugged terrain, and with the darkness came the same fears of the previous night, the same chilling foreboding, the same little jump at every sound. All around the camp the circle of little pagan sentinels, the multi-colored markers of the Yahrim, continued to stare in-ward with unblinking, angry eyes. The campfire crack-led and flickered, casting its dancing orange light on the explorers sitting quietly around it, waiting, not say-ing a word.

Dr. Cooper sat on a log, his chin resting on his hand, motionless. Jay and Lila lay nearby in their sleep-ing bags, asleep. Bill and Jeff sat on the other side of the fire from Dr. Cooper, a checkerboard set up be-tween them, a very slow-moving game in progress. Tal-mai Ben-Arba stood just outside the light of the fire, by himself, holding what looked like his rifle, silently guarding the camp.

From anywhere outside the camp, they appeared as a normal group of unsuspecting Americans with their local guide—with one difference: as the minutes passed, not one member of the party moved a muscle. Dr. Cooper sat there minute upon minute, his chin resting on his hand. Neither Bill nor Jeff made the next move in their game. Ben-Arba never looked this way or that.

Dr. Cooper was wearing a different pair of shoes, the ones that usually hurt his feet because they were still new. His other clothes were fresh out of his bag and not yet soiled with the desert dust. The only thing that looked the same tonight was that wide-brimmed hat.

That same old hat, resting on a head . . . stuffed with straw.

His body was of straw, stuffed into a spare shirt. His legs were spare tent poles and straw, as were his arms. His hands were an extra pair of gloves. He was a dum-my, deep in thought.

Jeff and Bill weren't really there either, and neither were Jay and Lila. Ben-Arba's hulking shape was very cleverly supported by an old snag of a bush.

In the rocks high above the camp, six very tense

human beings waited and watched in a long, silent vigil, rifles ready. Dr. Cooper and Ben-Arba were hiding directly above the camp. Bill, Jay, and Lila held a position about thirty yards to their right, while Jeff was hiding about thirty yards to their left. From these three positions, the camp could be viewed from a variety of angles—*nothing* could approach it unseen.

Dr. Cooper looked at his watch. "Eleven thirty."

"He'll show," said Ben-Arba.

Jay and Lila didn't have much to say. Both of them were thinking of the previous night and looking anxiously for any shadows that grew or moved. There were shadows everywhere, deep, black, and threatening, but none of them stirred or moved, except in their frightened imaginations. There were no sounds, but they'd already learned that meant nothing.

The night would soon be its darkest. The pagan markers all around the camp remained in place, serving their purpose, calling to the giant, leading him to this spot. The silence of the night almost seemed like a cloak for Anak Ha-Raphah to hide in. The darkness was his home, his world, his territory—and their enemy.

The day was their friend and protector, for the light seemed to chase him away, as it would any ghost.

But now it was night, and they all knew he would come.

# EIGHT

Ben-Arba looked at Dr. Cooper curiously and asked, "What is it you find so interesting at a time like this?"

Dr. Cooper was looking again at his writing pad. "I'm wondering if these words might help us out tonight . . ."

"Mm. The song Mara the Sorceress sang to you?"

Dr. Cooper nodded. "The syllables are familiar, but the words aren't complete. They don't make sense."

"Mara is a wicked woman. She is only taunting you with her riddles."

"But aren't you the one who told me to pay careful attention to every word she says? Every *letter* of every word?"

Ben-Arba was cornered. He looked away for a moment, sighed, and then answered, "If I know Mara, the words do mean something, but we may never know what."

"What about those other two words we talked about?"

"Eh?"

"Greed and power."

Ben-Arba hissed some air out through his nose and smirked. "What about them?"

"Why would Mara want to use those particular words in her riddles?"

"I don't know." That sounded very much like a lie.

Dr. Cooper decided to press a little further. "She must have had them on her mind for some reason."

Ben-Arba wouldn't look at Dr. Cooper but just kept fidgeting with his rifle. He finally answered very bitterly, "She is consumed with them both, Dr. Cooper. She hoards Anak's treasure, and she rules like a tyrant over the Yahrim."

"And yet," Dr. Cooper ventured, "she seems to have some regrets about it. Her riddle said that greed fills the heart of man, but he can never be satisfied."

"*She* can never be satisfied!" Ben-Arba countered.

"And as for power, maybe she has power over the Yahrim, but her riddle said power rules the one who has it. Do you suppose she was trying to tell me that all her power is ruling *her*?"

Ben-Arba nodded a slow, angry nod. "And who told you all this?"

Dr. Cooper took a small Bible from his pocket and began to thumb through it. "It's just a pattern, a simple truth from the Scriptures. Greed is a sin, and lust for power is a sin. Psalm 19, verses 12 and 13, says that sin usually starts out small, like our own harmless little secret. We might start with just a little bit of greed, or just a little bit of power, but that greed and that power just keep growing, and we keep wanting more and more, until finally we can't control them anymore— they control *us*. 'Let them not rule over me,' it says."

Ben-Arba looked down toward the camp, and his eyes became cold and vicious as he spoke: "Anak."

Dr. Cooper nodded with understanding. "Anak is ruling her, isn't he?"

Ben-Arba nodded slowly, reluctantly. "Anak rules them all, but not after tonight!" Then he added, "Your Scriptures must tell you everything!"

"Yes, that's true. As a matter of fact, I just happened to find your name in here."

"My name is not in your Hebrew book!"

"Sure it is—right here. Arba."

Ben-Arba put on a wry smile. "My name is *Ben-Arba!*"

Dr. Cooper smiled too. "The word *ben* means *son,* right? So your name means, Son of Arba."

"Your words are more aimless than Mara's riddles!"

"Oh, just stay with me now. There *is* a man named Arba in the Bible. He lived long ago, before Abraham, and if you go through some of the Scriptures that talk about who was the father of who, you find that Arba had a son named . . . Anak."

Ben-Arba became silent and glowering.

Dr. Cooper kept going. "Anak was the father of the Anakim, a race of giants, and his three sons were named Ahiman, Sheshai . . . and Talmai." Talmai Ben-Arba didn't say a word, so Dr. Cooper continued. "So Anak was the son of Arba, which makes me think that even though the Anakim called themselves after their father Anak, they could have taken the name of their grandfather Arba just as easily. Then they all would have used the last name, Son of Arba, or . . . Ben-Arba. These men in the Bible could be your ancestors."

Ben-Arba riveted his eyes on the camp below and held his rifle tightly as he growled, "I am not interested in your Bible lessons, Doctor."

"Oh, I just thought you'd be interested in how accurate the Biblical record is, seeing as your family name is so well-known in Gath."

"Your talking will spoil our trap!"

"Could I ask one question, though?"

"No!" Ben-Arba almost shouted.

Dr. Cooper offered the question anyway. "Why do you always wear those gloves?"

Ben-Arba's head spun, and he glared at Dr. Cooper.

But their discussion was suddenly interrupted. Both men jumped a little as a very familiar, very loathsome sound pierced the silence, then began echoing and growing all around them like the approach of death itself—*The Song of Ha-Raphah,* wailed and chanted by hundreds of unseen, fanatical Yahrim now hiding in the shadows, the crevices, the crannies, filling the hills all around them, singing one long, mournful wail upon another, like distant sirens, like crying goblins in the dark.

Dr. Cooper was astounded. "Where did they come from? We didn't hear a thing!"

Ben-Arba was impressed and a little shaken as he looked all around. "It could be they have learned to move silently, just as Anak does." He looked down at the camp, and especially at the ghostly pagan markers surrounding it. "Their ghost is haunting the hills this night, and they are calling him forth."

"Dad!" came Jay's voice.

Dr. Cooper turned with a start. He looked toward the campsite below.

"Dad!" came Jay's voice again, and he sounded desperate.

Ben-Arba could hear it too. "What . . . Is that your son, Dr. Cooper?"

Dr. Cooper looked dumbfounded. "Jay!" he called, trying to be as quiet as he could.

In reality, Jay was not at the campsite. He was still hiding with Bill and Lila and could hear his father calling him. He looked very quickly at the others. They could hear it too, and were just as surprised to hear Dr. Cooper break the silence.

"Jay, where are you?" Dr. Cooper called again.

Bill whispered, "You'd better answer him before he gives us all away!"

"Over here!" Jay half-called, half-whispered.

But Dr. Cooper heard a much louder voice calling from the camp—"Dad, I'm down here!"

Dr. Cooper was horrified. "Jay, what are you doing down there?"

"Dad, help me!" came Jay's desperate plea from below.

Dr. Cooper sprang to his feet. "I've got to go down there."

Ben-Arba was bewildered. "What are you doing? Do you want the Yahrim to see you? Our trap . . ."

"He's my *son!*" Dr. Cooper said, leaping over the rock that had concealed him and dashing down the hill.

"Do you want Anak to see you?" Ben-Arba protested. But Dr. Cooper was already too far away to hear him.


Jay could see his father running and leaping from rock to rock, racing down toward the camp, and he was flabbergasted. "What . . . what's he doing?"

"Jay!" Dr. Cooper called. "Where are you?"

Jay looked at Bill and Lila, and they were as puzzled as he was. He finally called out, "Dad! Dad, I'm up here!"

But Dr. Cooper couldn't hear him and kept running furiously down the hill.


Ben-Arba kept watching Dr. Cooper, not sure what to do, wondering what was happening. But then the answer occurred to him. "Mara . . ." he whispered.

He aimed his rifle toward the camp. All he could do was be ready.


Dr. Cooper stopped for a moment to listen. He was only fifty feet or so from the camp, where the fire continued to flicker and the straw campers continued to sit motionless.

"Dad . . ." came Jay's voice. "Hurry!"

It was coming from the temple of Dagon. Dr. Cooper looked all around, his gun drawn, as he hurried toward the voice of his son. He dashed from one concealing rock to another, looked here and there for any danger, then made some more quick dashes until he reached the crumbling temple wall.

"Jay!" he called.

"In here, in here!" came Jay's voice.

Dr. Cooper ducked through an opening in the wall and right into horrible darkness, one huge, black shadow cast by the temple walls. He kept his back against the wall and prayed his eyes would be able to see *something*. Above him, Dagon's loathsome face jutted above the shadows and appeared to float by itself in the moonlight.

"Good, good," came Jay's voice. "You came right away!"

Dr. Cooper froze in his place. He pulled back the hammer of his gun.

The voice was wrong. It had become higher, raspier. His stomach twisted with a horrible thought: *I've been tricked.*

"You love me very much, don't you?" said Jay's voice, but it was melting, fading into another voice. "Enough to risk your life, enough to ruin your trap?"

Dr. Cooper recognized the voice at last. "Mara."

The Sorceress whispered, "Come closer, Jacob Cooper, and don't make a sound. I have saved you. You must save *me!*"

"I can't see you."

Something moved in the corner. Her six-fingered hand jutted into the moonlight and beckoned to him. Now he could just barely make out her face.

"Come," she said.

"Step out into the light," he replied. "I don't trust you."

"You must! I need you—"

There was a gurgling, choking sound. The hand and the face vanished. Only silence remained.

"Mara?"

Hearing the hissing of falling sand, Dr. Cooper waited, keeping his back pressed tightly against the wall.

"Mara?"

There was no answer.


Ben-Arba heard something. He spun around.

"AWW!"

A body flopped to the earth right beside him. It was a woman. Silver hair. Long robe. He turned her over.

Mara the Sorceress.

In the sand, only inches away, were monstrous, six-toed footprints.

Ben-Arba's heart melted, and he screamed. He struggled with his rifle—where was the trigger? He couldn't think. He pointed the rifle here, there, up, down. He saw nothing. He kept screaming.


"Stay here," said Bill, leaving Jay and Lila hiding in the rocks. He ran to help Ben-Arba.

Jeff moved in from the other side.


Dr. Cooper could hear Ben-Arba's anguished cries and bounded back up the hill full-pace.


Jay asked Lila, "Can you see anything?"

"No," Lila whispered. "Where did Dad go?"

"I don't know."
"Stay down."

Ben-Arba was gripping his rifle, wildly pointing his finger at the footprints. Jeff had his rifle ready and immediately surveyed the entire scene.

"There's nothing here," he said.

Bill knelt by the fallen Mara. Something had attacked her. She was alive but dying.

Dr. Cooper reached the scene and was awestruck by what he saw.

"Mara!" he said, his face etched with horror. "How . . . how did you get here? What happened?"

"Anak Ha-Raphah . . . He is silent, invisible . . . He carried me like the wind," she said so very weakly. "Talmai . . ."

Ben-Arba knelt beside her and touched her face with his big gloved hand.

"Talmai, you were right," she told him. "I should have listened to you. Anak is no longer a son . . . He is now my *god.*"

"No, no more!" Ben-Arba said bitterly. "For doing this, he has brought punishment upon himself! He deserves to die, and he will die tonight!"

Mara shook her head. "*Nothing* can destroy him, Talmai, not even his powerful brother."

"If he is no longer your son, he is no longer my brother! He is our enemy, a curse upon us!" Ben-Arba looked at the others and tried to explain. "Mara the Sorceress . . . is my mother."

Dr. Cooper nodded. "And Anak Ha-Raphah is your brother. Bill asked some questions in Gath. We know."

Mara looked at Dr. Cooper. "I saved you, Jacob Cooper. Anak was here, right behind you like a shadow, and you didn't know it."

Ben-Arba's eyes were wide with horror. "No . . . we heard nothing . . ." With that, he looked again at the huge footprints.

"He is quick as a shadow, and he moves without sound, unseen, unfelt." She smiled a crooked smile. "But *I* could see him. I had to lure you away before he could reach you."

Dr. Cooper was puzzled. "Why save us, your *enemies?*"

She pointed to Dr. Cooper's Bible and answered, "You already answered that riddle, Jacob Cooper. You gave the answers before my throne, and I heard what you said to Talmai. You know who my real enemies have become."

Dr. Cooper understood. "Greed and power."

"Anak," answered Ben-Arba.

The old woman nodded at them both. "I do not care for you or your little band of trespassers. But your enemy is also *my* enemy."

"So Anak *is* ruling you," said Dr. Cooper.

"Just as you thought," she agreed. "At first he was my puppet, my power, my weapon. But before I even knew it, he became my ruler, my most horrible fear, and I could never control him again. When I saw you there in my chambers, I thought to myself, 'This man is bold and different.' I had to test you, and you proved to be a man of great courage and strength, a man who could challenge Anak and set us all free."

Dr. Cooper shook his head. "No. The courage and strength are not mine. They come from my God. *He* is the One who strengthens me."

She chuckled. "Then may your God save you and your children, Jacob Cooper. I am past saving." She gave her head a very feeble wag and said sadly, "Greed and power have finished me."

"Your own *son* did this to you?" Dr. Cooper asked in disbelief.

"My *god* did this to me. I made him angry."

Ben-Arba muttered, "He has become a devil."

"Is there *any* way we can stop him?" Dr. Cooper asked.

"The song, Jacob Cooper," she said. "The words I sang to you."

Dr. Cooper dug the writing pad from his shirt pocket. "But . . . they don't make any sense. They're only half there."

"There are two halves."

"Where's the other half?"

"One bird fallen, three captured, one flown; life for your children, carved in stone."

Dr. Cooper looked at the others. Another riddle!


"Jay!" came the voice of Dr. Cooper. "Lila! Get down here, quick!"

Jay and Lila both heard it. It startled them.

"What's . . . what's he doing over *there?*" Lila wondered.

"Something's gone wrong," Jay figured.

Dr. Cooper's voice called them again. "Hurry! You must get down from there! Do as I say!"

The voice was coming from behind them, down the far side of the hill.

"Dad, what is it?" asked Jay.

"Quiet! Just get down here, *now!*"

Jay and Lila got up hurriedly and moved toward the voice. They couldn't use their flashlights—their father had earlier told them not to—so they couldn't see Dr. Cooper at all.

"Dad!" Jay called as quietly as he could, "which way are you?"

"Down here," came the answer. "Don't make a sound—just hurry."

Mara was fading fast, and there was nothing they could do.

"The riddle, Mara," Dr. Cooper pleaded. "Please, just give us the answers!"

She smiled a weak, taunting smile and whispered, "So I must explain it? Then listen . . ."

Dr. Cooper leaned close to hear Mara's faint words.

Just then, Jay's fading voice came from around the hill, "Okay, Dad, we're coming!"

Bill heard it and muttered, "I told those kids to stay put."

Jeff waved a No signal with his light. "He knows better than that."

Dr. Cooper looked up. "What is it?"

"The kids. They must have thought you wanted them," said Bill.

But Mara's eyes suddenly grew wide and she gasped, "Your children!"


Jay and Lila hurried over the rocks, moving steadily down the hill.

"Yes, down here, down here!" came their father's voice.

"We can't see you!" said Lila.

"I'm all right. Just get down here before something happens! You're not safe up there."

They were heading down into a ravine. It looked familiar.


"What about my children?" Dr. Cooper asked Mara.

"*I* was the voice of your son . . ." Mara gasped.

"I know. It was a very clever trick."

She grabbed his arm in desperation. "The children are hearing *your* voice!" She gasped another agonizing, rattling breath and continued, "I knew you would risk anything for your children, and you did. But now Anak knows it too! *He* is calling them!" Her head dropped to the sand as she formed the name in a dying whisper—"Anak . . ."

She was gone.

Dr. Cooper sped over the rocks, followed by Bill and Jeff, their rifles ready to fire, their flashlight beams sweeping up and down the hillside. The Yahrim were singing louder now, wailing out a harsh, prolonged chant as if to frighten these men in their time of desperation. Dr. Cooper and his men tried their hardest to ignore them.

They reached the hiding place where Jay and Lila had been, but they were gone. They shined their lights this way and that, and finally found some tracks in the sand.

Jay and Lila were surrounded by the eerie singing and chanting of the Yahrim as they hurried along the trail, their hearts pounding, their hands shaking, their courage steadily draining.

They listened for the voice of their father, hoping they would still be able to hear it over the ghostly cries from the hills all around.

Then they heard it. "Come on—hurry!"

Jay hollered back, "Where are you?"

"Down here!" came the answer. "Follow the trail!"

Now Lila remembered this path. She'd followed it before. She held Jay back.

"Jay," she cried, "this is the trail to that pit where I found the goat!"

"Are you sure?"

Lila didn't have time to answer. Dr. Cooper was calling them again. "You kids hurry up! Do you want to get killed?"

They got moving. Their father must know what he was talking about.


Dr. Cooper, Bill, and Jeff raced along the trail, following the footprints of Jay and Lila.

Then Dr. Cooper dug in his heels and came to a halt. There, in the middle of the trail, was another set of huge, six-toed footprints. Some of the children's footprints were *inside* them.

"They're following him," said Jeff.


Jay and Lila had entered the ravine and were coming near the pit. They could see the demonic markers of the Yahrim surrounding that hole, the skulls grinning, the masks laughing, the ribbons and feathers waving like ghostly hands.

They stopped. Everything was the same as last night: the eerie singing, the still, oppressive air, the deep, dark shadows, the mocking skulls and staring masks. Lila looked up at the stars—the stars that had disappeared, one by one, behind the rising form of the ghost. Would they start disappearing again?

"Jay," she said, trembling, "there's something wrong about this."

Jay nodded. "I'm with you." He called, "Dad, are you there?" This time, there was no answer.


"Doc!" said Bill. "I think I can see 'em!"

They halted and strained to make out the forms of the children in the ravine below.

"It has to be them," agreed Dr. Cooper.

"They're right on the edge of the pit!" Jeff observed.

Ping!

"Get down!"

Ping! Plink! Arrows ricocheted off the rocks and skipped end over end along the ground. From above came the angry war cries of the Yahrim archers.

The three men crouched behind some rocks just as a spear whizzed overhead and nosed into the sand.

Bill aimed his rifle up the hill. "We'd better keep 'em busy." He fired a round over their heads with a deafening boom and a fiery flash.

"All right—they're taking cover," said Jeff.

It was the moment Dr. Cooper needed. He scrambled down the trail, crouching, dodging, dashing from cover to cover. Someone above spotted him, and another arrow just nicked his sleeve. Jeff must have seen the archer—his rifle shot echoed and rumbled through the hills.

"Jay!" Dr. Cooper yelled. "Lila! I'm up here!"

Jay and Lila spun around. Now *that* was their father's voice! They tried to dash up the hill away from that pit.

Too late! Suddenly, like an overturning table, the rock ledge they were standing on lurched upward, tilting crazily, pushed from beneath. It catapulted Jay and Lila into the air and they tumbled into the pit, landing in the soft sand.

The floor of the pit seemed to come alive. The sand began to move and sink under them, flowing toward the center like water flowing toward a drain. It was shifting, covering their legs and arms and drawing them toward a deep, sand-gulping hole that opened right in front of them. They struggled and squirmed and tried to kick, but the sand held them under its weight and they could not break free.

"Dad!" Jay screamed. "Help! Down here!"

Dr. Cooper was trying to reach them. A razor-sharp arrow zinged by his ear and he dropped behind some rocks, sliding, crawling, getting down the trail any way he could.

Jay held Lila's hand, trying to keep the sand from swallowing her up, but it was no use. He was being swallowed up as well, and there was nothing to grab, absolutely no way to stop it.

When Dr. Cooper reached the edge of the pit, the sand was up to Lila's neck. He flung himself on the ground and reached down.

"Grab my hand, Jay!" he shouted.

Jay groped for his father's hand, missed it, groped again.

"Help me . . ." came Lila's muffled voice as the sand covered her mouth and nose.

Jay caught hold of a few fingers with his free hand. He held tightly to Lila with the other. Dr. Cooper tried to get a firmer grip, but the sand just kept flowing down that hole, sucking Jay down.

Soon Lila was gone, and Jay was up to his neck.

"Lord Jesus, help me!" Dr. Cooper prayed. He could feel Jay's grip slipping as he was pulled over the edge of the pit.

Bill and Jeff made it to the pit and ran to help.

Jay shut his mouth tightly as the sand closed over his face.

Now his hand pulled loose, and Dr. Cooper groped for it, hanging far over the ledge.

Jay's head disappeared, and then, still waving and groping for his father's hand, his arm sank out of sight.

Dr. Cooper slid off the ledge and fell to the floor of the pit. The sand was still moving, but the hole was shrinking as the sand began to fill it. In a final, desperate attempt, he plunged his arm into that gulping hole in search of his son.

Jeff anchored himself on the ledge and held Bill's legs as Bill grabbed Dr. Cooper.

But there was no need. Dr. Cooper was kneeling, digging and clawing after his children, but the sand had closed in over the hole and had stopped moving. The hole was gone, and the sand was solid.

What was that? The anguished groaning of rocks against each other? The distant howl of a wolf?

It was coming from somewhere far below, filtering up through the rocks and sand.

Dr. Cooper looked up at Bill and Jeff, and they looked at each other, afraid to say what it really was.

But Dr. Cooper knew exactly what it was—the voice of Anak Ha-Raphah. The monster was singing.

He had taken the children!

# NINE

Zing! More arrows! Singing spears! Bill and Jeff tumbled into the pit to escape.

They looked for cover, then aimed their rifles. Dr. Cooper crouched against the rock wall and drew his revolver. Arrows were coming from all directions. The Yahrim were on every side of that pit, and there was no way out. They'd fallen into the perfect trap, and they knew it.

Unfortunately, so did the Yahrim. Immediately the men could hear a multitude of footsteps above the pit as the Yahrim boldly moved in. Then, just behind the grinning masks and skulls, the goat-skinned warriors appeared, their faces blackened with soot, their eyes full of hate and murder, their powerful arms brandishing bows and spears. There, at one end of the pit, stood the Hawk, and at the other end the Wolf.

At the Wolf's command, the archers drew back their bows and the spearmen raised their spears.

It was just like falling through an hourglass. Jay had lost his grip on Lila's hand, and now he was dropping through a rocky tube in inky blackness, surrounded and rammed along by a cascading stream of sand that threatened to smother him. He thought he heard a giant wolf howling.

Suddenly the tube emptied into open space, and he fell free for an instant before landing and rolling in a mound of soft sand, the stream of sand from above still pouring down on him.

Suddenly all was silent, and he couldn't see a thing. *Where am I?* He was about to call out for Lila when . . .

Hhhuffff! A hot, raspy breath poured over his neck.

His legs sprang like a trap, and sand flew everywhere as he leaped aside into the blackness.

Oof! He went sprawling over another body.

"Ow!" Lila yelped. "Jay?"

He grabbed her and helped her to her feet. "There's something back there! Run!"

They stumbled ahead in total darkness as Lila groped for her flashlight. She found the switch and shot the beam forward.

The monster was now in front of them. Two huge, yellow eyes glowed back at them from deep within the tunnel.

They slipped and slid to a halt, then scrambled the other way, racing along a meandering tunnel that seemed to have no end as it stretched beyond the beam of their light into a black void.

"Jay! Lila!" came Dr. Cooper's voice booming up the tunnel behind them. "Come back!" Then the voice deepened into the voice of an invisible devil. "Come back, Jay and Lila. Come back and face your *god!*" The beast seemed absolutely delighted with the thought, and laughed a loud, demonic laugh that seemed to make the whole tunnel shudder.

The Yahrim were ready to shoot their arrows and hurl their spears and Dr. Cooper was just about to order his men to fire. There was simply no other choice.

Then, from somewhere up above, a familiar, roaring voice bellowed in a foreign tongue.

The Wolf and Hawk looked up, hesitant with fear. Their hands trembled. Their spears sank toward the ground.

The other warriors spun and aimed in the direction of the sound, but they too stopped and, trembling in terror and muttering religious chants, lowered their weapons and started backing away.

The big, bellowing voice roared again, and the Yahrim dropped their weapons.

As Dr. Cooper and his men looked on in amazement, all the Yahrim dropped slowly to the ground, bowing their heads between their knees as if worshiping.

The whole scene was suddenly silent. Dr. Cooper and his men looked at each other in amazement.

Dr. Cooper had a guess. "Ben-Arba."

They could hear footsteps pounding down the path. Then, like a ghostly vision, a hand appeared, illuminated by a flashlight beam and held high, the fingers spread. As the hand approached the edge of the pit, their eyes followed the arms down to the face. It was Talmai Ben-Arba, his gloves removed, holding up his hand so all could see.

His hand had six fingers!

He shouted more orders to the band of warriors and they leaped from the ground, gathered up their weapons, and retreated from the pit.

"Come on out," he called to Dr. Cooper and his men.

Dr. Cooper, Bill, and Jeff scrambled quickly out of the pit, very glad to be alive.

"The Sixth Finger of the Anakim," said Dr. Cooper.

"Mara taught them to fear it above all," said Ben-

Arba. "It became her symbol of power. Since she ruled with her six fingers, so will I . . ." He looked quickly at Dr. Cooper. "At least until we can save your children."

Jay and Lila rounded a corner in the tunnel. It came to a dead end! Lila shined her flashlight behind them, but the beam could only reach so far. There was no telling what followed them in the darkness beyond the light's reach.

"What . . . what now?" Lila asked fearfully.

A voice mimicking Lila's echoed back at them from the depths of the tunnel—"What now, what now, what now?" Then it broke into that same hideous laugh.

Jay found a narrow passage to the side. "Let's go!"

They ducked through it, but they could still hear a deep huffing breath closing in.

Ben-Arba had the Yahrim under control. They stood at a distance in awe and reverence, gazing at his uplifted hand, waiting for his next command.

Ben-Arba growled in anger and heartbreak, "So this is where power and greed have brought us! My mother is dead, and now I command her subjects, a tribe of bloody savages!" He looked at Dr. Cooper and his two men. "So you've found me out, eh?"

"The people in Gath know about you and your mother," Bill answered. "And they've heard rumors about a . . . a monster born to your family."

"More than a monster. A *miracle,* something that had not occurred among the Anakim for thousands of years."

Ben-Arba barked some more orders to the Yahrim, who quickly picked up their weapons again.

"We can use them on our side now," he said, and

then he continued to explain. "We did not remain a pure race, but mixed with the Philistines and other races, and the giants were no longer born. But then, my father, who just happened to be a pure Anakim, married my mother, a pure Anakim, and though I, their first child, was like any other but for the sixth finger, the second child . . ." Ben-Arba paused and shook his head in horror and wonder. "Perhaps her witchcraft caused it to happen."

"She bore a giant," Dr. Cooper prompted.

Ben-Arba nodded. "When he was only nine years old, he was as tall as I am now; in her wickedness and greed, Mara named him Anak, nurtured him in her witchcraft, and raised him to be a monster she could use to terrify people and control them. What you said about sin, greed, and power are very true, Doctor. Anak became sin incarnate, a walking evil, and the Yahrim became his victims. Mara used him to terrify the Yahrim so she could rule over them and take total control of their treasures . . ."

"But then," Dr. Cooper ventured, "the power by which she ruled began to rule her."

"Anak became very skilled in violence and terror, as you have seen. Yes, at one time he bowed to Mara, his mother, and she commanded him. But no longer. He now believes he truly is a god. He is an uncontrolled devil, running rampant, subject to no one."

Ben-Arba peered into the pit as he gathered his next thoughts.

"He wants *you*, Dr. Cooper," he said finally. "He could have killed me when he destroyed Mara, but he didn't. You are the prize he wants. Mara did ruin his first attempt to destroy you, so now he is trying another, more horrible scheme." Ben-Arba looked at Dr. Cooper with eyes full of anger. "He knows you love your children. He is using them as bait to trap you."

"What will he do with them?"

Ben-Arba had no time to waste words. "He will taunt them and terrorize them, much as a cat plays with his prey. . . And then, whether he gets you or not, he will certainly kill them."

Walls, walls, walls! The tombs were a maze, with no discernible pattern. Jay and Lila kept running, with no idea where they were or where they were going.

"No!" Jay hissed as they came up against another dead end. "This tunnel used to go through—I *know* it did!"

"I thought so too," Lila agreed. "I've seen that carving before."

She was referring to another hideous carving on the wall, a violent, horrible event much like the pictures they had seen earlier. The conquering warrior, a beastly, wild-eyed figure, seemed to glare down at them from his high perch on the wall.

They stood still for a moment. They could hear nothing except their own desperate breathing. Lila shined her light here and there, afraid of what it might reveal. They could see the deep tunnel they'd just come through, but little else.

"Lila . . ." Jay whispered at last. "We're lost."

"I know," she admitted.

A sound. Lila clicked off her light, and they crouched against the wall.

It was coming up the tunnel so fast, it could have been a gust of wind. It passed, them, and they could feel the burst of air in front of it.

They were both thinking the same thing. It had passed them. They would double back the other way.

They rose from their hiding place and started quickly and silently down the tunnel in the dark.

HHHUFFF!

Lila went down hard, and her flashlight clattered across the floor.

Jay groped in the dark, trying to find her. She was kicking, crying out, struggling.

Something swatted him aside like a fly. He rolled on the floor and suddenly felt the flashlight jab his ribs. He clicked it on.

A hand! Jay ducked, but it wasn't as close as it seemed. Its size made it seem close. It vanished.

The light caught Lila and two monstrous fingers that suddenly released her. She pitched forward to the floor, got up again, and ran like a frightened animal, Jay right beside her.

Suddenly they noticed another passage to the left. They hadn't seen it before. They turned and ran down this new tunnel. They knew they couldn't run much longer.

"All right," said Dr. Cooper, "what now?"

Ben-Arba fretted and shook his head. "I . . . I don't know, Doctor. These tunnels . . . Anak has filled them with his own mysterious trickery . . . The pit of sand is something I have never seen before, something of his own invention."

"We can't get down that way, no sir!" said Bill.

"In other words," said Jeff, "we don't know which way to go to save Jay and Lila."

"While Anak knows every tunnel, every hiding place, every trick!" said Ben-Arba. "Dr. Cooper, if your God is so great, you surely need His help now."

Dr. Cooper was already praying—earnestly. Bill and Jeff joined him and there was an awkward moment as the three men huddled together, heads bowed. Ben-Arba stood there watching.

Then Jeff looked up. "Doc," he said, "I think the Lord's given me something. What about Mara's riddle?"

Dr. Cooper latched onto that immediately. "That has to be the key." He took out his writing pad and looked at the meaningless words again. "What was that last riddle she gave us, the one that rhymed?"

Ben-Arba recalled it. " 'One bird fallen, three captured, one flown; life for your children, carved in stone.' "

"Oh, Lord," Dr. Cooper kept praying, "please help this thing to make sense!" Then, just as in Mara's throne room, an answer came to him. " 'One bird fallen' . . . That could be Jerry Frieden."

" 'Three captured, one flown' . . ." mused Ben-Arba. "Yourself, Doctor, your two children, and me."

"Our encounter with the Yahrim in the tombs. I and the children were captured, but you escaped. That has to be it!"

"Keep goin', Doc, keep goin'!" said Jeff.

Dr. Cooper strained to think. He prayed again as he reviewed the riddle. " 'Life for your children, carved in stone' . . . Carved in stone, carved in stone . . ." His prayer was answered. "The inscription?"

"What inscription?" Ben-Arba asked.

"In the tunnel, right beneath the ventilation shaft! It didn't make any sense. Letters were missing. And it had been etched in the wall recently."

"Ahh! As Mara said, the riddle is in two halves! One half you now hold in your hand . . ."

"And the other half is in that tunnel!"

"The other escape route I followed!" said Ben-Arba. "I remember it. Come!"


Jay and Lila had to rest. Lila clicked off her light, and they slumped against the cold stone wall in a passage. Which passage it was, or where it went, they had no idea.

"Jay and Lila Cooper . . ." came an eerie, thundering voice from somewhere in the maze of inky black passages, echoing off the walls.

The children froze. There was simply no way to tell where it was coming from.

"It is useless to try to run from me," said the voice. "At every moment I hold you in the palm of my hand."

Jay gripped Lila's arm and whispered, "Don't answer him. He might be trying to get our location."

There was another hideous chuckle, and then the voice went on, "But hear me. There is a way to keep your lives. Give them to me. I am the only god with whom you have to do. Worship me, and you will live."

Jay and Lila knew they could never worship him. They remained silent.

Anak Ha-Raphah spoke again. "Worship me, and your lives will be richer. I will share my treasures with you." There was an ominous pause, and then, in a threatening tone of voice, the giant warned, "Refuse to bow down to me, and you will die."

Jay took hold of Lila's hand and prayed very quietly, "Lord Jesus, You're the only God we'll ever serve. Please help us out of this mess. Help us to think. Show us what to do."

"Amen," said Lila.

They stood there silently for a moment, surrounded by nothing but cold and blackness, with no sense of direction and no idea how close their enemy was lurking. But as they remained still, they could sense God giving them peace and speaking to their hearts. They began to set their minds to the problem.

"I think . . . I think he's teasing us. He's trying to wear us out," Jay whispered very quietly.

"And I think we're letting him."

"So we've got to stop running and *think*. We've got to outwit him somehow."

"But he can move so quietly. We never know where he is."

"And he knows his way around down here and we don't."

"But I don't understand these tunnels. It's like they *change.*"

"Either that or we're really confused. Listen, let's do that maze trick we learned."

Lila thought for a moment and then said, "It's a start."

"Come on."

Jay placed his hand lightly against the wall, and they started walking very carefully and quietly.

Some time ago Dr. Cooper had shown them that most mazes can be solved if you place a hand against one wall and never remove it as you walk through the maze. They were going to give that a try.

The route had been tight, winding, and difficult, but now Dr. Cooper, Ben-Arba, Jeff, and Bill had reached the tunnel directly beneath the ventilation shaft. Ten gallant Yahrim warriors were with them, now under the command of Ben-Arba, a "holy" descendant of the Anakim.

"Here it is," said Dr. Cooper, and several lights shined on the strange-looking marks on the wall. "I was sure this was a recent inscription. Mara must have known that outsiders would first enter the tombs at this point."

"Ehh . . ." said Ben-Arba, "and this is her own bizarre way of calling for help."

Dr. Cooper took out his writing pad and began to mutter the words and sounds to himself, following each line of the inscription with his finger.

"Right!" he said to himself. "That would fit there perfectly, and that . . . and that . . ."

He began to scratch out some more letters on the wall with his pocketknife. The letters and words from his writing pad began to fall into place in the gaps in the inscription.

"It looks like a poem of some kind. Mara's creation, I suppose."

"She always was one for little rhymes," said Ben-Arba.

"Here's one complete line." Dr. Cooper began to carefully sound out the strange, foreign words.

Just then, one of the Yahrim warriors responded, exchanging glances with his fellows and pronouncing some of the words himself.

Ben-Arba exclaimed, "Doctor, he knows the rhyme!"

Ben-Arba grabbed the warrior and drew him near. He pointed out the letters to the man, and the two of them began to chatter away in the Yahrim language.

"Doctor," said Ben-Arba, "he says the next line should begin with . . ." Ben-Arba pronounced the word.

Dr. Cooper checked his writing pad, found the word, and wrote it into the space in the inscription. With the warrior's help, another line, then another, and finally the last one were completed. The two halves of Mara's riddle were put together.

Ben-Arba looked it over and explained, "A simple rhyme, Doctor. It will not rhyme in English, but it could be translated: 'Who can stand before the sons of Anak, we count twelve and twain are we, I am wise and fill the earth, I have fled and tread the earth, riches to one and not the other, who can stand before the sons of Anak?' The rest is a family lineage, names of our fore-fathers. Not much of a poem, and I'm afraid it tells us nothing."

"She was writing about her two sons," Dr. Cooper observed. "Sons or descendants of Anak, who count twelve . . . Their number system is based on twelve instead of ten because of the twelve digits on their hands. One fills the earth. That would be Anak, down here in the tombs. One has fled and treads the earth . . ."

"And that would be me," Ben-Arba realized.

" 'Riches to one and not the other'?"

Ben-Arba nodded regretfully. "Riches I came to steal, Doctor. Mara and Anak knew of the vast treasures of the Yahrim, hidden somewhere in these tombs by generations of Philistine sea raiders. With Anak's help, Mara took control of the Yahrim and hoarded their treasures."

"And I hear they booted you out," Bill added.

Ben-Arba looked at Dr. Cooper. "Greed again, Doctor. They had taken the treasure for themselves. They didn't need me—so they drove me out with not so much as a trinket. I vowed I would have my revenge—I would take it back from them!"

"And you thought you'd get us to help you?" asked Dr. Cooper.

"I could never steal it back by myself. But when I saw you and your group come to this place, I thought to myself, 'Ah, here are the people I can use to help me find that treasure!' "

"Greed, once again," said Dr. Cooper in disgust.

"An ugly sin, Doctor."

"We'll talk about it later," said Dr. Cooper, returning his attention to the inscription on the wall. "Right now, my children's lives depend on the answer to Mara's riddle. It has to be somewhere in this poem."


Jay and Lila kept moving through the tunnel, one hand always touching the wall. They had gone for hundreds of feet, then turned some corners, then doubled back, then found another passage, followed it, then turned some more corners. They were beginning to wonder if they were getting anywhere at all when they finally began to see a faint orange glow ahead of them.

They stopped for a moment, listened, heard nothing. Maybe the thing was following them, maybe not.

They had no way of knowing. They continued toward the glow.

The tunnel sloped downward. They finally saw a large doorway up ahead with an orange-lit room just beyond it. This looked familiar.

A thought occurred to Jay, and he stopped.

"Turn on your flashlight and let's check these walls," he whispered in Lila's ear.

Lila clicked on the light and slowly swept the beam over the walls of the tunnel. The light glimmered off something just ahead. Jay pointed, and she returned the beam of light to that spot.

They both knew what it was: a snare. They could just barely see the fine, silver thread stretched across the tunnel.

Jay stepped forward very slowly as Lila lit his way. He followed the thread to where it disappeared into the wall. Then he found what he was looking for.

Lila came up behind him. "What is it?"

Jay moved very carefully, very slowly around a small niche in the tunnel wall, trying hard not to disturb anything. Lila came closer with the light and finally saw the glimmering, razor-sharp tips of six arrows, mounted on a tightly drawn crossbow, hidden very cleverly in the wall.

"I'll bet *he* rigged this up!" Jay said.

"Just look at the size of it!"

"Come on."

They ducked very carefully under the thin, almost invisible wire and worked their way down the tunnel toward that room.

Yes, they had been here before. It was the ceremonial room where they'd first encountered the Yahrim holy men. The bonfire in the center of the room was now down to smoldering embers. The room was silent and sinister.

Jay was encouraged. "Good. All we need to do is

find that cave entrance the Yahrim took us out through and we're out of here!"

"Let's go!"

They proceeded—slowly. Lila shined her light up and down ahead of them as they looked very carefully for snares. So far, so good.

A vast collection of huge, hideous weapons hung on the wall: a spear at least twelve feet long, many blades of all shapes and descriptions, chains, arrows, and also a deadly, curved sword the size of a door, with a shining, razor-sharp edge. Such a sight only made them want all the more to get out of this horrible place.

Where was that cave entrance? Jay was sure it had to be at this end of the room, but so far they just couldn't see it. They hesitated and started looking around.

"I'm almost sure it was this way," said Jay.

"I think so," said Lila. "I remember those shields hanging up there. It was just past them."

"Okay. Keep an eye out behind us."

Lila froze and grabbed Jay's arm. He looked, and she pointed toward the wall of weapons.

The sword, that deadly, curved sword the size of a door, was *gone!*

"Jay . . .!"

Instantly she was on the floor, knocked aside by her brother's body.

SLAM! The sword came down in a flashing arc. Weapons, stones, chips of wood and metal went flying.

No time to think. They dashed across the room as the sword rose high in the air, held by a menacing, unthinkably huge hand.

The dull glow of the smoldering fire gave them only a vague outline of the giant, an incredibly huge shadow that seemed to fill the room. They could see the reflection of the fire's light on the edge of that blade; they could see the dull yellow reflection from those demon eyes.

"Jay!" Lila shouted.

They leaped aside just in time as the sword came down like a bolt from a thundercloud and sparks flew from the rocks. Lila ran one direction, Jay the other. The giant was laughing thunderously as he went after Lila, stepping over the firepit in one easy stride. She was cornered. Jay found a large hunting blade and threw it with all his strength. The blade glanced off the giant's thigh. He did not turn, but the blow threw his aim off. The edge of the sword zinged over Lila's head and chopped through some wooden shelves, turning them to splinters as iron weapons clattered and clanged to the floor. The giant stumbled, off-balance. Lila ran around him, ducking into some shadows, circling the room, looking for her brother.

She spotted him. He waved frantically, and she joined him. They ran for the tunnel they'd taken into the chamber.

With one flying leap, the giant was there, waiting.

# TEN

It had to be the Lord. A thought raced through Lila's mind and she acted, beaming her flashlight into the giant's eyes.

His big eyes shut with pain for just an instant, but that was enough.

They sneaked past him, ducking into the tunnel. Lila was ready to turn on the speed, but they had only gotten a short distance into the tunnel when Jay grabbed her, pulling her into a dark shadow around a corner of the wall. He let out a scream that frightened Lila at first, but then she understood his plan and screamed as well. Then they froze there in the dark, not making a sound.

The dull, orange light from the room blinked out: the giant had entered the tunnel. He was racing toward them with incredible speed and silence.

They prayed—only a few words, and the monster passed them with a gust of wind. Then, out of the darkness came a *zipzipzip*, a roar of pain, and a loud metallic clatter as the big sword hit the tunnel floor.

The snare had struck its inventor!

Jay and Lila bolted and ran the other way, toward the big room. There had to be another way out.


"Yes!" Dr. Cooper said excitedly. "That's it!"
The others gathered for a close look.

"Look here!" Dr. Cooper said, pointing to each place in the inscription. "This line intersects this one, and both lines share this letter where they cross."

"Like a crossword," said Bill.

"The same thing happens here, and here, and down here . . . *Twelve* times altogether!"

"Twelve," said Ben-Arba, "the Anakim lucky number!"

"Twelve different letters," said Dr. Cooper, "appearing in this inscription in a particular order, with no letter ever being repeated."

"Keep goin', Doc, keep goin'," said Jeff.

"Here's the first letter, right up here. And look over there at that wall!"

They all looked where Dr. Cooper was pointing. On the opposite wall, just a short distance down the tunnel, was a large carving of the very same letter, a little squiggle on top of a short, vertical stem, like a crude flower.

"Test that wall," Dr. Cooper instructed.

Jeff and Bill took a close look but didn't see anything unusual about the wall. Ben-Arba examined it for himself, tapped it with the handle of his knife, made a face . . . and kicked a hole right through it!

"Ha!" he bellowed. "You have discovered something, Doctor! The wall is false!"

Dr. Cooper began to hurriedly scribble down all twelve letters he'd found in the inscription. "All right now, there are inscriptions and letters inscribed everywhere, all over the tombs. But if my theory is right, *these* letters, followed in the same order as they appear in this inscription, should mark the path through the tombs to the treasure."

Ben-Arba barked orders to his new warriors, and they began sliding the false wall aside.

"So how do we find Anak?" Bill asked.

" 'Where your treasure is, there will your heart be

also,' " Dr. Cooper quoted from the Bible. "Anak's lair has to be near his treasure. That's the place to start."

The Yahrim warriors had uncovered a passage behind the false wall, and Dr. Cooper led the way.

Jay and Lila ran around the ceremonial room, looking for another way out. The passage to the outside simply wasn't there, and the tunnel they'd used the other day was still sealed shut with that huge slab.

They could hear a dragging, clanking sound from the tunnel they'd just come through—the giant was coming back!

Jay looked up toward the smoke hole in the roof. "Boy, if only we could fly!"

"Hey, what's that?" Lila asked, pointing.

Halfway up the wall was a small, round hole, possibly another ventilation shaft.

The giant was getting closer. He was limping and no longer silent, but moving *fast*. They had no time to spare.

There was a narrow ledge beneath the hole, but it was too high to reach from the floor.

"Jay, how about that spear?"

They ran to where all the weapons were displayed, grabbed the huge twelve-foot spear, and leaned it against the wall, point down. Jay gave Lila a boost to help her on her way, and she shinnied up the spear far enough to grab the ledge and pull herself up.

The monster burst into the room like an angry bull, still wielding that huge sword, his leg wounded and bleeding.

Jay scrambled up the spear and reached the ledge just as the giant spotted him.

Lila had reached the hole and tumbled through it. Now she reached out to lend Jay a hand.

The beast came at them with footsteps that shook

the whole room. Jay leaped for the hole and slithered through it just as a hand plunged in after him.

Jay and Lila rolled down a narrow shaft and out of reach as the hand groped this way and that, reaching deeper and deeper.

"Where does this shaft go?" Jay wondered.

They started crawling to find out.

Dr. Cooper found the next letter among many others, over a doorway. They all passed through it, ran down a short tunnel, and came to a large room filled with pottery, old tapestries, and clay jars that undoubtedly contained ancient scrolls. It was an incredible discovery for any archaeologist, but Dr. Cooper paid no attention to it now. He was looking at the three other tunnels leading out of the room. All of them were marked, but not with the next letter on his list.

"Now what?" asked Bill.

"It has to be here somewhere," Dr. Cooper answered.

Flashlight beams darted all about the room.

"Doctor!" said Ben-Arba. "There, in the floor!"

Dr. Cooper saw the large squiggle. "That's it! That's the next letter. So far, so good."

They converged on the spot, moved a heavy wooden panel aside, and discovered a large opening with a steep stairway leading down.

They all dropped through the opening and raced down the steps.

Jay and Lila crawled, slid, and scurried down that long, narrow shaft and finally came to an opening into another room.

Lila shined her light through the opening. "Oh-oh."

The opening was about ten feet up the wall of what appeared to be an ancient burial vault, the walls and floor a very dusty, dingy gray, the air very stale and very dry. Dust-laden spiderwebs formed lacy tapestries in every corner, and in the center of the room, on immense, rectangular slabs, lay the withered remains of four Anakim, dressed in their massive armor, their swords at their sides. They must have been powerful generals when they were alive. It was clear to see that they had to have stood at least ten or eleven feet tall. One bony hand was visible—it had six fingers.

"Boy, if Dad could see *this!*" said Jay.

Lila shined her light here and there, searching around the room. "This place must have an awfully high ceiling . . . I can't see it."

"And I don't see any way out, either. They must have sealed this place a long time ago. Wait a minute—what's that over there?"

Lila held the light still, revealing a large wood and bronze crank mounted on the opposite wall.

"Remember that door to the ceremonial room—the one the holy men tried to trap us with? This could be the mechanism for another one of those sliding doors," said Jay. "A trip lever drops it, but you raise it with a pulley and a crank."

"So where's the door?"

"I don't know. Maybe a part of the wall comes up."

"I wonder . . ."

"Wonder what?"

Lila's eyes were wide and shifted about as she thought things through. "Remember how the walls in those tunnels seemed to change? We could never figure out where we were."

Jay could see her point. "Hey . . . And the same thing happened the first time, when the holy men were chasing us. We thought we'd taken the wrong tunnel. But . . . you figure Anak was raising and lowering walls just to confuse us?"

"Yeah . . . something like that. So maybe we were never as lost as we thought we were."

"But why would he do it . . ." Then a thought occurred to him. "Unless he's herding us—you know, cutting off every route except the one he wants us to follow."

"So he must know where we're going to end up no matter which tunnel we choose. He must want us to end up somewhere."

"Unless we fouled up his plans by ducking into this little shaft."

"But he has to know where it comes out." Lila peered down from the opening. The floor was quite a drop below them. "What do you think? Should we try for it?"

They looked around the room some more. It was deathly still.

"Quiet as a . . . well, a tomb," said Jay.

"Well, I don't know what other choice we have. Let's go."

"We'll make a chain."

Jay, anchoring himself in the shaft, hung onto Lila's hands so she could lower herself as far as possible. From there, she dropped to the floor. Jay crawled out, hung from the opening by his fingers, and dropped to the floor with a landing roll.

They moved quietly past the dry, gray skeletons on the slabs as if they were afraid of disturbing these giants' three-thousand-year sleep.

Jay wasn't tall enough to reach the crank. "Eh . . . people were taller back then. C'mon, I'll give you a boost."

Lila set her flashlight on one of the slabs, the beam trained on the crank. Jay linked his fingers and made a stirrup for her foot, giving her the extra height she needed to grab hold of the primitive wooden device.

She pulled, but the crank wouldn't move. She pushed, and it eased slowly over.

"You're doing it," said Jay. "There's a crack under the wall now."

"This is going to take a while."

"Hurry."

Lila heaved on the crank with all her strength, and it began to rotate slowly, ponderously. The wall began to rise little by little. The crank loosened up and turned more easily, and Lila turned it faster. It took several turns to lift the wall even an inch.

"It's coming, it's coming," said Jay excitedly.

Just beyond one of the gray, dusty slabs, a small drop of red appeared on the floor, then another, then another.


Dr. Cooper and company came to the bottom of the stairway and found themselves in another tunnel. Flashlights played on all the walls, looking for the next letter, a squarish shape with a dot over it.

A Yahrim warrior shouted and pointed.

There it was, about twenty feet down the tunnel and near the top of the wall.

Ben-Arba tested the wall. "A panel of some kind. I think . . ."—he began heaving on it sideways—". . . it will move aside."

The others grabbed on and pulled. It began to move.

"Another tunnel," Dr. Cooper reported, shining his light through the opening. He was getting a bit discouraged but couldn't give up.


Lila kept cranking as the dust of ages trickled off the crank and into her hair. The wall had risen about a foot or two.

"How're you doing?" Jay asked.

"Getting tired, brother," she said.

Jay thought he heard something. "Shh."

They froze.

There it was again. A drip. Then another tiny drip.

Lila dropped silently to the floor. Jay grabbed the light and pointed it toward the sound.

They only saw the circle of blood on the floor for an instant.

BOOM! A giant, six-toed foot pounded to the floor, and a cloud of dust exploded upward as the room was suddenly filled with a sweating, bleeding, towering shadow.

Jay and Lila scurried and squirmed like frightened mice under the slightly raised wall panel and had just cleared it when the huge body slammed against it and another hideous laugh shook the tombs. They raced down the dark tunnel with no idea where it would take them, and had not gotten far before they heard the wall panel shatter into thundering, tumbling fragments as Anak burst through it.


"Did you hear that?" Dr. Cooper asked.

They all had.

"It must be Anak!" said Ben-Arba. "We are getting close!"

They ran down the tunnel they'd found. They passed another tunnel entrance with no letter to mark it, but something else did catch their eye—drops of blood on the floor, a trail of them leading out of the side passage and down the tunnel they were following.

"Somebody's been hurt, but who?" Dr. Cooper wondered aloud, his face etched with concern.

They ran ahead, now following the red drops. Suddenly their light beams began to cut through a haze of recently raised dust.

"Careful," said Dr. Cooper.

Just ahead of them, the tunnel had no floor but dropped directly into a burial vault. Four Anakim warriors lay there in repose upon four huge slabs, their fleshless jaws grinning up at the rescue party. The Yahrim warriors yelped and backed away from the sight, full of fear.

Ben-Arba understood. "This is a very sacred place to them, Doctor. They cannot approach it."

"But we'll have to," Dr. Cooper replied. "Take a look."

Dr. Cooper's light had cut through the dusty haze and found Letter Number Ten in the sequence, right above a monstrous hole that had just been broken through the wall. More bloodstains were clearly visible on the floor of the vault.

"He had to have come this way, and evidently dropped into that room."

"Then we're right on his tail!" said Bill.

Dr. Cooper could also see the footprints of his children in the dusty floor, tracked over in many places by the huge, six-toed, bloodied prints of the giant. "He's the one who's bleeding, but he's right behind Jay and Lila!"

Jay and Lila ran and ran, the cold, stone walls of the dark tunnel racing past them endlessly, the footsteps of Anak Ha-Raphah pounding behind them like a steady, relentless pile driver, shaking the floor, rumbling like approaching thunder.

"He has us just where he wants us," Jay gasped.

"Wherever that is," Lila answered.

They soon found out. They could see light up ahead, growing brighter. They were coming to another room, and now they could see large, flaming torches upon the walls, filling the room with a flickering, yellow light. They burst from the tunnel into that room and immediately looked everywhere for another avenue of escape. They could see none.

This had to be their final destination, the very place Anak had been forcing them to go. They were surrounded by gigantic furniture: a monstrous bed, a towering table, a chair big enough for a dinosaur, stonecutting tools it would take two men to lift, several knives that could fillet an elephant. A fireplace the size of a garage was cut out of one wall, and a large fire was still smoldering.

They had entered the giant's lair, his home beneath the earth!


The Yahrim would not continue the chase, no matter what Ben-Arba told them. They wouldn't even look upon the four Anakim giants that lay in the vault below.

"Let them stay," said Dr. Cooper. "But I need their mantles and scarves!"

Ben-Arba barked the command, and the Yahrim tossed their goatskin mantles and woven scarves to Dr. Cooper, who began tying them into a crude rope.

"All of you, hold this end," he said to the Yahrim, and Ben-Arba translated the order.

As the Yahrim waited above, Dr. Cooper, Ben-Arba, Jeff, and Bill slid down the rope one by one, their blood racing, their hearts ready for a battle.


Anak was coming down the tunnel toward his lair like a roaring train.

Jay ran one way and Lila the other. They circled the room in opposite directions, looking for any passages, any hidden doors or panels, *any* way out.

There seemed to be no way of escape.

Death itself was closing in. The Fearsome One had just come through the doorway.

They were stunned at the sight of him. Now, for

the first time, he stood in enough light to be entirely visible. He was massive, his body was muscular and heavily forested with hair, and he stood incredibly tall. His eyes were like the crazed yellow eyes of a demon. His hair was black, tangled, and long. He wore a wide, leather belt across his chest and the ancient armor of the Anakim about his hips.

At the sight of the two trapped children, the big, bearded face broke into a jagged grin.

But suddenly a loud cry echoed out of the tunnel behind the giant. "Anak! Stop!"

It was the voice of Talmai Ben-Arba! The giant heard it and leaped clear of the doorway just as the tunnel behind him echoed with the thunderous boom of Ben-Arba's rifle. The shot pinged and sparked off the stones near Anak's shoulder.

Jay and Lila could see beams of light playing deep in the tunnel, and then Lila cried, "It's Dad!"

For just a brief moment they could see Ben-Arba aiming his smoking rifle, Dr. Cooper at his side.

But Anak had seen them too, and with eyes full of hate and cunning he grabbed a trip lever in the wall beside the doorway. With the whirring of pulleys and ropes, and the grating of stone against stone, another huge slab began to drop into place.


"He's closing the door!" said Dr. Cooper.

The four men ran toward the doorway, now slowly blinking shut like a big eye, cutting off the light of the room from the tunnel. It started dropping faster, and the men sprinted toward it desperately.

Too late. With a thud of finality, the slab came to rest on the tunnel floor. The four men now found their way blocked by a solid wall of stone—a wall etched with a very large, almost mocking image of Letter Number Eleven.

# ELEVEN

The giant was quite pleased with himself and laughed at the plight of the men he'd trapped outside his lair. The huge sword came out of its sheath once again, and he eyed Jay and Lila with a wicked stare.

But the drop of the slab had sent a puff of air through the fireplace, and Jay noticed a small flurry of sparks blowing into some kind of space behind the fire.

"Grab on!" he shouted to Lila, and the two took hold of a sheepskin rug, held it in front of themselves, and ran toward the fireplace.

Anak came after them, not quite so swiftly this time, limping on his wounded leg, bracing himself against the big table, the big sword lifted high.

The kids took a flying leap, let the rug land on the smoldering coals, covering them, and sprang in a somersault over the fire, tumbling into the cavity behind it. They rolled down a shallow chimney of stone and landed in another fireplace on the other side. With a burst of gray ash and a scattering of cold, charred logs, they rolled into another room, this one also lit by huge torches on the walls.

Lila came to rest on the stone floor and looked up just in time to see Jay rolling near a fine wire only a foot or so from the floor.

"Look out!"

Jay bumped the wire and instantly the floor right next to him collapsed and fell through with a tremendous rumble. He rolled away just in time. Now there was a deep, yawning pit in the middle of the floor, a trap big enough to catch a dinosaur.

Some rocks and pebbles plinked and rolled down from the wall above and the children froze. Lila had just barely touched *another* wire. They looked toward the disturbance and could see a large slab of rock high up the wall, teetering on edge, held there by wooden poles and ready to drop with the tripping of the wire.

"This place is *full* of traps!" Jay exclaimed.

"Lord Jesus, help us!" Lila prayed out loud.

Dr. Cooper spun around. "Lila!" he said.

Bill and Jeff shined their lights toward the ceiling. They also had heard Lila's voice.

"Doc!" said Bill. "Right here! It looks like another ventilation shaft!"

They all looked at the small opening in the ceiling of the tunnel. They could hear the voices of Jay and Lila coming through it, very faint, very distant, echoing through the long, rocky tube.

"Wherever the kids are," said Jeff, "this will get us there."

Dr. Cooper dropped his gun belt. "Give me a boost."

Ben-Arba himself was able to thrust Dr. Cooper into the opening. Dr. Cooper squirmed his way into the narrow passage and reached down for his gun.

Bill handed it up to him. "Go ahead, Doc. We're right behind you!"

The room was spooky and ominous. There were several more hideous, bloody carvings on the walls, illuminated by the flickering yellow light of the torches. The masks and charms of the Yahrim were everywhere, mocking, threatening, staring at them. Besides all that, pebbles and shards of stone were still dropping now and again into that deep, dark pit in the middle of the floor, and the huge stone high on the wall was still teetering as if it would crash down on them any second. There were no doors or escape routes visible—nowhere to run. There was a small opening for another ventilation shaft high on the wall, but no way to reach it.

Wait! Nearby, another crack was opening near the floor. A slab was raising! The giant was coming through a hidden door!

Jay and Lila looked everywhere, but there was no place to hide. They could think of only one chance to take. They ran to the opening door and waited right beside it, pressed against the wall.

Dr. Cooper held his gun in front of him as he squirmed and wriggled through the narrow tunnel like a mole, desperate to get to his kids. He had no idea what he would find or what he would do when he got there, but that was in the Lord's hands. His task was to *get there.*

The door raised quickly and finally yawned to its full height, almost twenty feet. Jay and Lila could hear the monster approaching. They could see his shadow coming through the door.

It was now or never. Jay interlocked his hands and gave Lila a boost.

The giant was one step from the door when Lila jumped and barely grabbed a large trip lever on the wall.

The giant stood in the doorway just as Lila hung from the lever and pulled it down with all her weight.

With a sudden roar of ropes and a grinding of stone, the huge slab dropped like an avalanche on the giant's shoulders, driving him to the floor and pinning him there as the big sword clattered out of his hand.

Jay saw his opportunity, ran over, and grabbed the big sword, dragging it along like a large plank toward the pit.

Anak Ha-Raphah tried to move, groaning, groping, gasping huge gusts of breath.

Jay reached the pit's edge. It was so deep he couldn't see the bottom. He tried desperately to pull the sword to the edge, to throw it in.

Anak's roaming hand found a large rock.

"Jay!" Lila screamed.

Jay didn't see the rock coming. It struck him in the right shoulder and he went tumbling like a tenpin, stunned and senseless, unable to see anything but a spinning blur. He thought he saw the pit under him, he could hear his sister screaming his name.

His mind clicked back on, and he knew he was falling. He grabbed the edge of the pit with his left hand, and his body dangled there over absolutely nothing. His right shoulder was numb and bleeding. He couldn't move that arm.

Dr. Cooper could hear Lila's scream echoing through the ventilation tube. He knew he was getting closer and pushed ahead with even greater determination.

Anak put his arms under himself, arched his back, and pushed up against the slab. It moved. It could not stop him, could not hold him. He pushed some more, got up to his knees, gave a mighty roar and another push, and he was *free*.

Lila ran to the edge of the pit, where she could see Jay dangling from the edge. She tried to grab him but couldn't reach him. The shadow of the giant fell across her. She leaped and rolled aside as the sword came down like a meat cleaver.

She darted away, heard a terrible crash, and turned.

Anak was on the floor again, bleeding, wheezing, injured, but glaring at her with those fiery, hate-filled eyes.

"You . . . will . . . *worship* me!" he growled in pain and fierce anger.

"No!" Lila shouted defiantly, even though terrified. "There's only *one* God, and He can beat you any day!"

"Then let Him *try!*" Anak roared.

He rose from the floor again and took two steps toward her. He buckled and sank to one knee.

She ran toward the other side of the room. He flattened out on the floor and shot out his arm, tripping her with his finger. She rolled on the floor, got up, and ran some more. His leg swung around and came at her like a rolling log, flipping her off her feet. She smacked her head on the stone floor.


Light! Dr. Cooper could see light ahead. He could hear Lila's struggle.


Jay was losing his grip on the pit's edge. He tried to hold himself up with his feet, but the rocks kept breaking away under him. He prayed. It was all he could do; it was the best thing he could do.

Lila was dazed. Her world was tilting and rolling all about her. She was cornered now, with no way to escape, and all she could see was black hair, dripping sweat, and those crazed, murderous, yellow eyes.

Dr. Cooper crouched in the opening. He could see everything. His mind raced to find an option, an answer.

Then he spotted it, right across the room from him on the opposite wall: Letter Number Twelve. By now he could recognize the hidden panel, and his eyes quickly darted to a huge weight suspended from a rope that went over a pulley: a counterweight!

The big hand wrapped around the sword's handle. The mouth pulled into a devilish, ruthless grin, so close that Lila could count the giant's crooked teeth.

Dr. Cooper pulled back the hammer of his gun, took careful aim, and fired.

The bullet sparked through the hook holding the counterweight aloft, and the huge weight began to drop toward the floor as the rope raced through the pulley.

The huge panel began to rise.

Anak heard the panel grinding upward behind him and looked over his shoulder in alarm. Lila took her chance and dashed around him, racing toward the pit to help Jay.

Anak spun quickly and awkwardly, looking for her through sweat-blurred eyes. But he was also looking toward that rising panel going up like a curtain, unveiling what appeared to be the light of a million sparkling stars.

"No . . ." rumbled out of his throat like the roar of a lion.

Dr. Cooper saw his chance. The giant was below him, between him and the opening panel, stooped over in pain. With a powerful leap, he launched out into midair and landed on Anak's hair-covered back. Anak lurched at the impact, and Dr. Cooper sprang once again through the air toward that door, landing right in front of it.

So this was it! The fabulous treasure! Jewels, diamonds, gold—all glittering in a dazzling display!

Anak didn't see Dr. Cooper. His wicked eyes had turned again to his little blonde prey, now courageously trying to save her brother.

Lila lay prostrate on the floor and reached into the pit to help Jay, but this cost her precious time and narrowed the distance between her and the advancing giant. Before she knew it, his huge hand pinched the tail of her coat. She kicked and struggled, but he snatched her up like a toy, ready to finish her with one stroke of that sword.

"ANAK!" Dr. Cooper bellowed.

Anak turned his ugly head, rolled his big eyes sideways, and saw Dr. Cooper for the first time. His mouth pulled into a hateful sneer, baring his jagged teeth.

Dr. Cooper stepped out boldly. "*I'm* the one you want! *I* am the intruder of your tombs!"

Anak stood there, huffing and wheezing, glaring in amazement at this litte man's daring.

Dr. Cooper reached into a huge chest and grabbed up a gigantic ruby. "And as for this treasure, it isn't really yours at all, is it? You've only hoarded it, keeping it from its rightful owners!"

The big hand shook with fury. The fingers opened,

and Lila dropped to the floor where she scurried away to safety.

Dr. Cooper could see he had the furious giant's attention. "And you call yourself a god! The one true God looks down from heaven and *laughs* at you!"

Anak raised his sword, and with a bellow that shook the walls, he began to close in on Dr. Cooper.

"Dad!" Lila screamed.

But Dr. Cooper could see the incredible greed in Anak's eyes, and he was ready. At just the right moment, he flung the beautiful stone high into the air, right in front of the giant's face.

The ruby fell toward the pit. Anak let out a horrible scream and dove headlong after the flying ruby, catching it in his outstretched hand.

The pit was waiting for him. His huge body came down like a giant tree, and only his free hand could reach beyond the far edge of the pit to the floor, groping desperately for a handhold, a way to save himself.

The hand tripped the invisible wire, and then vanished as Anak dropped into the chasm with a final roar of hate.

High on the wall above, wooden poles flipped aside, rocks and pebbles popped out of their places, and the huge slab of stone began to fall forward. Dr. Cooper ran toward the pit, sprawled on the floor, and groped about in search of Jay's hand.

The stone hit the floor with the force of an earthquake and then keeled over toward the pit. Its shadow fell across Dr. Cooper as he found Jay's hand. Dr. Cooper gave a tremendous, desperate yank.

The stone was dropping. Dr. Cooper and Jay went tumbling, sliding, and rolling out of the way, and the stone slammed down over the pit like a mountainous lid. Loose rocks from the walls bounced and rolled across the floor. The impact knocked two torches off the walls. The air was filled with dust. The crash of the stone became a long, ringing roar that echoed around and around the room until it finally faded.

The Coopers were together on the floor, huddled and holding each other. They moved not a muscle until all the sound had died away.

After almost an hour, Jeff finally made it through the ruined ventilation shaft and found the Coopers still alive and in one piece. He didn't disturb them, not yet. They were still sitting together on the floor, offering a prayer of thanks for being alive. Jeff found his way back to the lair's entrance, operated the mechanism, and let Bill and Ben-Arba in.

Before long, Dr. Cooper and Ben-Arba were examining the huge stone that now covered the deep pit.

"Anak's handiwork," said Ben-Arba solemnly. "A monstrous trap, a ridiculously huge snare . . . All to protect his loathsome treasure!"

Dr. Cooper couldn't help recalling a pertinent Scripture. " 'He who digs a pit will fall into it . . . He who rolls a stone, it will roll back on him.' "

Just then, Jeff and Bill came in from Anak's lair, and Dr. Cooper knew what they were about to report from the looks on their faces.

"You've found Jerry Frieden?" he asked.

Bill nodded. "He didn't make it, Doc."

Ben-Arba looked down, and his whole body started to tremble. For the first time since Dr. Cooper had known this big, powerful man, tears appeared in his eyes. "Sin is such a deadly thing, Dr. Cooper. How many people have been hurt by Anak's greed? How many of the Yahrim have lost all they cherished because of his lust for power? And now . . . now sin has taken my mother, and One-Leg, and your Mr. Frieden . . . and even destroyed its greatest servant, my brother."

Dr. Cooper figured this would be the best time to say it. "The Bible says that sin can only result in death, Talmai. but there is an answer. Sin doesn't have to rule over you; Jesus Christ can wash it away. He has broken its power."

Ben-Arba wiped the wetness from his eyes and said, "The Yahrim need a leader who can guide them out of their poverty . . . and out of their ignorance." Ben-Arba looked at his six-fingered hand and shrugged. "I suppose they will be looking to *me.*" Then he added with a deep sincerity, "But they need to know *your* God, Dr. Cooper. They need a God who is real, who is loving, who truly cares for them and does not use them for His own gain."

Ben-Arba looked at Dr. Cooper and asked, "Doctor, is your God like that?"

Dr. Cooper smiled. "Yes, Talmai, He is. And He's a *giving* God, not a taker. He loves us all and gave His only Son to take our punishment for our sins, and to give us a new life, an eternal life. All we have to do is believe in God's Son, Jesus, and accept Him."

Ben-Arba thought about that, then said, "If you have the time, I would like to know more about your Scriptures, and about your powerful God, and about His Son."

"It'll be my pleasure," Dr. Cooper replied.

"But what will you do now?"

Dr. Cooper looked at his children and his two men standing nearby and answered, "Well, I guess we'll get back to doing what we came for. There *is* a wealth of knowledge in these tombs. I guess now we have time to go back and take a look at it."

Ben-Arba smiled. "And I now preside over a tribe of people who know these tombs well and who owe you their assistance." He offered Dr. Cooper his big, six-fingered hand. Dr. Cooper took that hand, and they shook on it.

With that, Ben-Arba and the Cooper party all headed toward the tunnels that would take them back to the surface.

"Incidentally," said Dr. Cooper, "after you tell Pippen and Andrews that the treasure is on the Yahrim's land and legally belongs to *them,* how do you intend to break that news to the Yahrim?"

Ben-Arba put his finger to his lips. "Shh. I intend to do that very quietly, and only when the time is right. Right now, my people are hard-working, virtuous, and spiritually hungry for the real God." Ben-Arba smiled with new insight. "When they have learned what true *spiritual* riches are, I will tell them."

"You know, Talmai," said Dr. Cooper as they moved up the tunnel, "I think you're going to do just fine."

With the pathway clearly marked, it took just a short time to reach the surface, and now it seemed so very easy to step out of the darkness below and into the light of day.